LINE

LINE

NIALL BOURKE

TRAMPPRESS

First published 2021 by Tramp Press
tramppress.com

A CIP record for this title is available
from the British Library.

1 3 5 7 9 10 8 6 4 2

Tramp Press gratefully acknowledges the
financial assistance of the Arts Council.

Thank you for supporting independent publishing.

ISBN 978-1-9162914-2-3

Set in Caslon and Frutiger by Marsha Swan
Printed by by L&C Printing Group, Poland

For Mum and Dad

It is not from the benevolence of the butcher, the brewer, or the baker that we expect our dinner, but from their regard to their own self-interest. We address ourselves not to their humanity but to their self-love, and never talk to them of our own necessities, but of their advantages.

— Adam Smith, *The Wealth of Nations*, 1776

I made a mistake in presuming that the self-interests of organisations, specifically banks and others, were such that they were best capable of protecting their own shareholders and their equity in the firms. Those of us who have looked to the self-interest of lending institutions to protect shareholders' equity (myself included) are in a state of shocked disbelief. I'd been going for 40 years or so with considerable evidence that it was working exceptionally well.

— Alan Greenspan, Federal Reserve Chairman, 2008

I

MORNING

And always before dawn come his mother's calluses.

Willard feels her leathered palms scratching at his shoulder, rousing him. He smells the billy-fires. *Morning again*, he curses.

– Up, up, she says. Water. And the roof too, while you're about it. Up.

Willard tries to roll off, to disappear back into his ragged excuse for a blanket. Her hands disappear and he thinks he has won – but then she whips the blanket away, leaving him shivering in his shirt under the dirty tarpaulin.

– Are we moving? he says, eyes still shut. I'm not getting up if we aren't moving.

– No, says Mother, walking away.

He listens to her steps, can picture the corner of the blanket caught in the crook of her elbow while the rest trails down through the ochre dust.

– But I've heard rumblings, she says. A big shift. And coming soon. Very soon. Maybe today.

– That's what you said yesterday, says Willard.

– Hush, she says. Up.

Willard lies still, trying to hug himself back to warmth but attempting to keep the heat inside himself is like trying to stop water escaping a sieve – whatever bit of his body he wraps in his arms only makes the rest feel colder.

He gets up, pulling one elbow over his head, then the other, an attempt to wring out the stiffness pooled in his back.

DRESSING

Dirtandshitandroutine.

Put on his jeans before the cold can cut strips off him, hopping from leg to leg to spare his feet. Throw on his other shirt and then grab his boots, making sure he undoes the laces rather than standing his feet into them because he knows the back and forth of his heel causes the leather to pull away from the sole. Last time Willard's boots fell asunder he was barefoot for near on two weeks.

Break the skin of ice on the water bowl – four below for it to form this thick – and brush his teeth with a finger. Catch a nut of water between cupped hands and douse his face, the trickles running down his neck until his chest clamps and forces out his breath like a clouded ghost. Dust off his burlap mattress-sack, roll it into a tight cylinder around the blanket and tie both in place with the frayed length of blue twine. Stack it all in the corner of the tent with the water bowl so everything is ready. Just in case.

Just in case the Line moves.

Just in case It moves.

Just in case It ever moves.

THE TENT

Willard shares the tent with Mother.

Inside is a stove and a red plastic basin acting as the sink. Stacked beside the basin on a rough-hewn plinth, as neatly as possible, are some cooking utensils: two tin plates, two mugs and bowls, two de-handled pots, a frying pan, a spatula with a snapped lath, a blackened long-handled fork and a collection of ladles in varying states of rust. The stove is no more than a hollowed earthen pit covered by a chimney, and the chimney is no more than a rudimentary pipe made from a series of lightweight metal cylinders. Each cylinder is narrower than the one before, so Willard can slot them together to form a funnel, the end of which he pokes through the tarpaulin to take the smoke away.

Willard knows something about the stove – it shouldn't be used for cooking. The stove is only for warming the tent when the nights become unbearable. Trying to cook on it gives off so much smoke that their eyes stream – so the cooking must be done outside on the billy-fire. And Willard knows something important about the chimney too – that he must coat it in a retardant layer of powdered gypsum wherever it might touch the tarp. More than one family has woken to the vengeful hissing of melting plastic dripping down upon them.

Or not woken, choked in their sleep by the fumes.

WATER

Willard stoops out through the polythene flaps of the tarpaulin.

Their tent has a grey roof, pitched ten degrees from high-side to lowest purlin, and a patchwork of walls hanging on a frame of the misshapen wooden poles. These tarpaulins are new coverings, light and flimsy, but Willard can still remember the old ones, the heavier ones that warped the frame. The older coverings were oiled canvases, mottled with mould and chequered by repairs and, although warmer, they had proved too heavy to carry on entering the foothills.

Willard knows the futility of trying to straighten a curved wooden pole. Hours by the fire, anchoring both ends in the earth so he can push down to unbow the middle – but it always dislodges, rotates rather than straightens. How is it that a framing pole can warp out of shape so easily, but never be bent back? Hours and hours. The pole still bent. The Line never moving.

He checks the roof for moisture, to prevent the water pooling until it hangs down upon them like a distended stomach. He has learned now not to displace the water the lazy way – by pushing up from below with a stick. Now he knows the stick's small surface area pushes the water outward, shaping the pool on the roof into a hollowed ring with the peak of the stick tenting up through the middle. Now he knows that continuing to push splits the tarp and down come gallons of water on everyone and everything inside. Mother didn't speak to him for days when it happened, not until he had dried all their sodden materials and paid further penance by washing the pots for the rest of the week.

Yes, Willard knows it is better to climb up on a barrel every morning, to bail out any water with a bowl and to save it in the drum near the fire.

LATRINES

Once Willard finishes clearing the roof, he gets down from the barrel.

Hanging by its handle on the far side of the tarp – away from the entrance – is the small latrine shovel he shares with Mother. The head of the shovel is covered in a fungus of rust, bumpy and heavily stained, and the splintering handle is held loosely in place by two corroded nails. Willard walks around to collect it and, with shovel in hand, makes out for the latrine pits.

The pits are set away from the tent-line, out past the new rubbish-trench, which Willard and the other young men helped excavate when the Line had last stopped. The open trench now marks out the Line's innermost perimeter, the area that must be kept sanitary, and as tempting as it might be for Willard to cut his walk short by squatting behind a rock, he knows he cannot.

Pissing is tolerated in the clean-zone, overlooked if done far enough away from the tents and then rinsed down, but both Mother and Mr Hummel have drummed the importance of using the latrine pits into him, subjected him to countless warnings of sections further down the Line that have been disembowelled by dysentery.

But, for all their stories, the walk is still long on cold mornings, the rocks still enticing.

Willard went in the rocks once before – but Mr Hummel caught him, jeans around his ankles, and hauled him up to standing by an earlobe. Then Mr Hummel thrashed him raw with a tinder-stick before waddling him unceremoniously back through the camp, thighs bare and bleeding. Willard spent the rest of the month on latrine duty digging other people's shit-holes – and he knows he won't get away so lightly for a second offence.

Willard crosses through the earthen-ridged waste-land of the old rubbish-channels and, after taking a wide step across the open trench, proceeds to pick his way through the sprawling collection of stone cairns which mark out all the shit-spots too recent to be re-dug. The Line hasn't moved for so long now, at least six ration-drops, and so every time Willard comes out here he must scour for longer to find a place to squat. The old holes, the really old ones, from the people cycles and cycles up the Line, no longer need any markers because the shit inside them has broken down, petrified to a harmless and powdery chalk. But if Willard loses patience, digs too close to a fresh-laid cairn, then the putrid smell when his shovel bites the earth is enough to keep him looking.

At last he finds a small clearing.

He digs a little, stops, sniffs and, satisfied, keeps digging some more. Then, checking the hole is the required depth of the shovel-head, he empties his bowels with a moan – hoping the single sheet of card in his pocket will this time be enough.

SMOKING

On the way back Willard stops by the rubbish. He takes the remains of a battered matchbox out of his back pocket and, hunkering down against the wind, sifts through the undulations of filth – rags, cans, rusted springs, squares of moulding hessian, tattered bags and tarpaulin sheets too shredded to salvage, leaking canisters and battered cartons – until he finds a suitable scrap of paper. Blowing it clean, he folds it by scoring between finger and thumb and then gums along the crease, tears off a length. The rest he folds into his pocket for later.

He waits for the wind to die and, when the rectangle of paper is sitting still, opens the matchbox. Pinching up the grum of tobacco, he sprinkles in a little under half, smoothing the yellowing strands with his index fingers before rolling up with his thumbs and licking along the edge to seal it in. He puts the narrow end in his mouth and, still hunkering against the wind, lights a match with a sulphurous grind. The head is damp, bubbles in the lee-shadow of his cupped hand before flaring, and Willard, eyes closed as the green spectre of the match floats over his retinas, pecks his roll-up in and out of the flame until he gets the tobacco to take. There he stays, squatting among the rubbish as the smoke tumbles up towards the grey knuckles of the morning.

All is still.

How long before they move again, how long before a new cycle? Spring is coming but the mornings are still cold, too cold, too cold until past midday when the sun climbs over the rocky ridges. And too cold too the cloudless nights, too bitter when out for a piss under the savagery of the stars.

When will they move? When when when?

MR HUMMEL

Willard smokes as he returns, and the Line comes awake.

All his life he has Lined Up one place in front of the Addison family and he hears them going through their morning ritual, the two children sitting by their billy-fire and squabbling like egrets as Mrs Addison assembles breakfast.

All his life he has Lined Up one place behind Mr Hummel, who now has his tarp stripped and folded and is lying supine on his mat chanting out his matins. Every morning Willard has watched Mr Hummel pray, and every evening too. Mr Hummel always lies in the same position, flat on his back, legs bent a little and both hands pulsing up his thighs then easing back down. All the while he sings out in a rhythmic wail, incantations now echoing back on him as if the very rocks of the valley are giving reply.

But Mr Hummel doesn't always finish his prayers in the same way.

On the days when the Line fails to move, which is most days, Mr Hummel stands up without a word and folds away his hessian prayer mat before pouring out a capful of water from his battered canister as a libation. And all the while something blows the corners of his mouth up into a smile, some wind of certainty that the failure of the medicines of his faith lies only in the dosage.

But rarely, oh so rarely, the Line does move – and then Mr Hummel's closing routine is different. On those days he still folds his prayer mat without a word but, before opening his water bottle to make an offering, he turns to Willard and Mother and he speaks.

– See? he says, shaking a finger above his head. See? The Emperors answer if we but learn to ask. We must but learn to ask. Maybe tomorrow you will join me in asking?

– Tomorrow, Willard replies, understanding his part in the pantomime. Tomorrow, Mr Hummel, I will pray with you tomorrow.

Then Mr Hummel smiles and disappears, leaving Mother sucking in air through the cadavers of her teeth.

– Why must you vex him? she says. He has Lined Up in front of us since before you were born. He has watched over you when I have been ill and has helped changed your shit-cloths. You used to think it an honour when

17

you were picked to help carry his belongings ahead of the other boys. You owe him some respect.

– I will pray when you do.

– I pray. Do you not hear the psalms my fingers sing every morning when rousing you from your sleep-sack?

– And what do they sing for?

– For you, Willard, for you. That you will live to see the end. They sing always for you.

SCHOOL

Willard still remembers the mornings spent in Mr Hummel's hedge-school.

He would cram beside the other children, on a bench made from a rough plank balanced across two stones, hands wedged between his knees and breath clumping as he intoned the morning address. *The Line has existed longer than anyone knows,* they would chant from memory as Mr Hummel would circle them, left hand held behind his back and his right punctuating their drawls with the curt flicking of a birch switch. He would continue to orbit as they chanted, examining the disjointed monotone of their words.

Our parents before us, and our parents' parents before them, have sacrificed everything so that we *may be where we are today. We owe it to them all to get to the end. Or at least to get closer; then may it be our children who continue our journey.*

After this, Mr Hummel would plant his sun-stick into the earth. The children would be called up, one by one, to demonstrate how they might mark the dirt around it to chop the day down into hours – and then they would all recite the rules:

1. *No one hast ever left the Line, nor shalt thou. To do so wouldst dishonour the sacrifices of all those gone before.*
2. *No one hast ever left the Line, nor shalt thou. To do so wouldst mean thy family must pay your penance.*
3. *And, anyway, there is nothing out there but rock-bears.*
4. *And thou wouldst most certainly be eaten by rock-bears.*
5. *Thou mayst wander until dawn and thy things shall not be stolen. (But thou shouldst probably pay someone to watch them, just in case. The Emperors are bountiful and the Emperors are fair, but let us not make their jobs more difficult.)*
6. *Thou mayst wander until dawn – but shouldst thou not be back come sun-up then thy place shall be the forfeit.*
7. *Thou mayst leave thy place in the Line but only once – when thou dost marry. But thou can only move down the Line, never up. For that is how thou will know it is true love.*

8. *And because moving up would be skipping.*

9. *And that is the most important rule of all.*

10. *Thou Shalt Not Skip The Line.*

11. *Thou Shalt Not Skip The Line.*

NYLA

Nyla sometimes wonders about moving down the Line when she marries, about giving up her place to cram in with Willard and Mother. Losing so many places is not to be taken lightly, but there are two reasons she knows it is right.

The first happened last summer, ten days after Nyla came into Willard's tarp and her face hung by a wide smile. But whatever distant possibility had been heralded by those early signs – the missed period, tender breasts – it left with little more than a trickle of blood, so quiet and quick she almost missed it. No cramping, Nyla told Willard afterwards, no pain; just a light spotting of bright red as some tiny thing inside surrendered its precarious grip on her womb.

That time, the first time, their loss was muted. Neither Willard nor Nyla had really accepted she was pregnant.

Outwardly they had acknowledged it, of course, laughed about how little sleep they would have, but neither had truly understood that they were to become parents and all which that might entail. In the days afterwards, they were painted with a sadness, but a moist one, and one which soon evaporated to leave behind a more pragmatic residue – a coating which reassured them that everything was, in fact, normal again; that they had been right all along in their continued suspicion that Nyla's pregnancy was too strange to be believed.

But the second time was different. It happened three days after Nyla had counted thirteen weeks. And this time they *had* come to think they were having a child. Really having a child. They had been cautious during the early stages, guarded, knowing something could go wrong, but as the days passed they allowed themselves to relax, to plan for what lay ahead. They had begun saving tinder-sticks to fashion into a crib, talked with Mr Hummel about the ceremony, about securing an additional stipend and moving Nyla's tent down beside Mother's.

But late one night the bleeding started. At first it was a smear of dark mucus and Willard, half-asleep, had muttered reassurances when Nyla had woken him; that it was probably this or most likely that. But it grew, heavy and bright. By the morning Nyla was filling strips of cloth as quick as Willard could cut them, sopping great sponges of clots the colour and texture of diced meat. Mother and Mr Hummel were called, rushed in with clothes and pans of warmed water, and the next day was one terrible stretching of uncertainty measured by the pauses between the long horrors of changing blood-soaked blankets, by wracking cramps and the filling of pots with seeping cloths as heavy as the silence coiled in the corners of the tarp.

Nyla's body recovered, although it took her a week of lying down and using Mr Hummel's poultices to kill an infection. The Line had been stationary. She was lucky.

And over the coming months she recovered her other places too. Through a force of love she reached out, found Willard once more, reconnected with him when staying together would have smothered those who loved each other less. Then, holding tight together, they picked out a path of drying islands from the receding waters of their grief.

Yes, Nyla sometimes wonders about moving down the Line when they marry.

But she knows it is right. And Willard knows it too.

STICKS

Willard's cigarette is a wet-end when Mother comes into view.

She carries a full bindle over her left shoulder and she drops it beside the remains of last night's fire with a whump. After erecting the iron tripod, she bends to her knees and blows deep into the embers, so deep her face is soon lost behind a squall of ash. The flames skulk back like cats, then spring up. Once the fire is no longer in doubt, she sits back on her heels and, without stopping to wipe the grey streaks from her face, takes the sticks from her bindle and starts snapping them between the knurls of her fingers. After each break she casts them onto the fire and there she stays, snapping away like a forgotten clock, her eyes tacks and the backs of her hands hawsers to choke the throat of the morning.

Willard finishes smoking and goes over to the fire. He picks up the empty water pail from behind Mother, turning it upside down. Some of the ash has mixed with the condensation formed inside, so Willard slaps the base with his palm to dislodge the resulting sludge, each beat of his tattoo ringing out and then breaking on the stones around his feet. Five slaps and he spins the pail back around to look inside. Satisfied, he leaves to draw the water.

During the last cycle, before the foothills, the Line had run parallel to a narrow stream. Drawing water there had been easy, but they lost it on entering the higher lands and now water is allocated, as always when they enter arid country, from stipends to be drawn from the communal vats. Willard considers saving himself the effort by just using what is in the drum by the fire – but they still have a stipend to collect and he knows Mother would chide him for such an extravagance.

He returns minutes later, the pail held out from his side so it doesn't knock against his thigh and spill freezing water down his legs. When he reaches the fire, he levels out a circle of earth with two rotations of his foot then lowers the pail on top, nudging it forward with a knee so it tilts on its bottom edge towards the waiting billy-jug. Despite his care, some of the water trickles onto his fingers and he feels a scorching cold above the top knuckles – but he keeps his hands in place until the billy-jug is full and the pail reverted to standing. Finally, he lifts the jug and loops its wire handle over the steam-clouded hook of the tripod, taking care not to burn his fingers.

The billy-jug boils with a spluttering whistle and Willard pulls his shirt-sleeve over his hand, folding it back on itself to thicken the cloth, then lifts the jug from the tripod. Mother has already stood their mugs beside the fire, a screed of coffee coating the bottom of each and, leaning his head back to escape the steam, Willard pours in the water. It clambers up the sides with a tinny burble as the bitter smell of coffee fills the air.

Beside the mugs is a small parcel wrapped in a dirty muslin cloth, which Willard opens to reveal a hunk of black bread and the dregs of a sticky-sided tin of condensed milk. He bites a lump from the bread, giving the rest to Mother and, chewing, prises the lid off the milk – at least up in the foothills there are no ants in it – and drips one glob into each of the coffees before handing a mug to Mother. He clamps two hands around his own, savouring the warmth of the metal, and takes his usual place by the fire, hunching low over the rising steam. He does not tell Mother the reason they need more coffee – that he traded most of what they had left for a snook of tobacco some days back, replacing what he had taken with a few pinches of dust so not to arouse her suspicion.

He still drinks the coffee – it doesn't taste much different. Maybe it had been cut with dust to begin with.

– You will need to walk up the Line after breakfast, she says. We are due a drop soon. Mr Hummel thinks so.

Mr Hummel is able to work out the intervals of the ration-drops somehow. Once Willard entered Mr Hummel's tarp to return a dowelling rod and saw hundreds of tally marks scratched into the earth, all but the last three lines crossed through diagonally to form a series of five-bar gates. Mr Hummel had seen Willard staring and had started to explain – how the ration-drops follow the moon somehow, but the cycles of shifting and stopping seem more erratic, tied to something else – but following his explanation hurt Willard's head and so he had not allowed himself to understand.

– What's he paying?

– Chits.

– The pap would be better.

– Maybe. But if the rations do come then the chits will be good. And Mr Hummel thinks we are definitely due a drop.

Predicting the rise and fall in the value of the chits that are traded up and down the Line is indeed a dark and mysterious art. After a drop, when goods are plentiful, the chits are worth more and can buy most about anything. If someone demands five chits for a bag of pap, then their neighbour could be usually be talked into selling for four. But when a drop is due, or overdue as is more often the case, goods are scarce and the value of the chits plummet as they flood back into the Line. Then people are willing to trade any number of them for even tiny amounts of food, and so a bag of pap can not be had for less than fifty.

It's a skill that has always evaded Willard, but Mother is able to predict the swirls and undulations in their value with uncanny precision. He has seen her hungrily gather chits before a drop was due by selling away precious rations – only to later buy back ten times what she had sold after the rations arrived. Other times, he has watched her refuse to do anything but barter for months on end, deliberately holding back her piles of chits to drive their price up. Once he even thought he had seen her burn some, a bid to take them out of circulation and so permanently raise the value of the ones she had left.

– I have to watch Mr Hummel's space later, says Mother, he needs to go down the Line to name a newborn. Be back by midnight.

She pulls out a slip of paper bearing her signature and another with Mr Hummel's, hands them over to Willard.

– I will find us that food, he says.

TRUDGING

As Willard trudges up the Line, he sees its landscape change.

It has now been stopped in the foothills for so long that an uneasy permanence has taken place. He passes the stalls and work stations people have set up; shacks where you can get your boots repaired in exchange for a bag of pap, stalls selling small drams of oily whiskey distilled from makeshift stills, or flat-breads blackened over a barrel-fire, places trading tin mugs or tarpaulin squares. As he walks he watches, sees the ubiquitous blue oilcloths give way to striped yellows and greys, sees after another hour's walk that stalls are trading an earthy-grey soup instead of the blackened flat-breads. He smells the smoke of the fires, feels it become acrid, sharper in his throat from the odd orange leaves families are burning to ward off mosquitoes.

Mr Hummel says the rest of the Line is ramshackle. Mr Hummel says they are lucky not to be Lining Up elsewhere; he tells stories of barefoot children running wild through forests of tented guy-ropes, or of latrine pits spilling unwisely close to water drums while men drink whiskey and lie against the rocks. *We are lucky*, Mr Hummel says, *lucky because our section is well ordered.*

There is a Council made up of Elders, like Mr Hummel and Mother, who oversee the running of certain things: distributing water when the vats are running empty, ensuring people use the pits, allocating rations so each family can be certain they will receive a fair supply for the month. And Willard agrees. The Council *does* work well. Punishments are rare. The last he remembers was a year ago, when Mr Addison got de-rationed for forgetting to close the tap on a water-vat. Rare but severe. Rare because they are severe.

Willard looks for signs of such disorder as he ventures up the Line. He can't see many – but he is not to be fooled.

He has heard what the Elders whisper when they think no one is listening: stolen rations, beatings over half a cup of pap, people murdered for their boots.

THE YOUNG WOMAN

Word of the ration-drop travels and before long even the slowest are on their way.

Willard is joined by many others – mostly young like him, stout-legged and resilient to their blisters – but some he sees are old or weak. He passes them, the shuffling men, the shambling women, infirm hunched backs foostering with empty bindles or trying to re-adjust biting shoe-straps. Many, having forsaken their own canisters due to the weight, plead softly for a drink – and Willard helps where he can: a splash of water, a pat on the back or some easy cajoling words. But he never tarries long, always keeping an eye on the climbing sun. He will be slower coming back with the three full bindles, even slower again should he get caught by the dark – and failing to make it back by dawn means his place will pay the forfeit.

It is not long before Willard falls in beside a woman who, like him, is carrying multiple packs. She is not old and decrepit. She is young and lissom. She is wearing shorts, her legs wiry and tough-looking. Their paces match and soon the silent rhythm of their strides fall in, syncopate, and they begin talking to pass the time.

– Did you see that woman? says Willard.

– An hour back? she says.

– Yes, says Willard, she was crying.

The young woman's speech quickens, the strange joy of having a sad story to tell.

– It was Mrs Elber. She was my up-neighbour but one. Her husband wandered from the Line last night, but he didn't make it back in time. He got lost, they said. Hunting for lizards.

– You still have lizards here? says Willard, incredulous. He hasn't seen any for months, thought them all long scavenged.

– I didn't *think* so, says the young woman. But he must have been tending a secret nest, way out in the rocks. They said he drank too much and couldn't find his way back.

She takes a mouthful from her canteen and re-threads the lid without breaking stride.

Willard wonders how drunk a man must be not to spot the fires of the Line burning through the dark. Even half-blind you'd see them from miles off. Very, he concludes. Very drunk indeed. The young woman keeps talking.

– Mrs Elber raised the alarm this morning, before sunrise, and the Elders sent out a search party. I saw them return as I was readying to leave, dragging in her husband's body on a catafalque. Well, the remains of his body. The rock-bears had got to him.

Willard opens his own canteen, drinks two small sips. As he replaces the lid he wonders what it would be like to die out there on those silent, empty plains.

– It was sad to see her mourning, says Willard.

– Mourning? No.

– Then what?

– She was giving thanks.

– Thanks?

– Yes, because the Elders showed her mercy. By rights they should have burned everything she owned for allowing a loved one to lose their place. But instead they granted her clemency, because she'd raised the alarm early. They only burned her husband's possessions; her things were spared.

Here the young woman trails off, breaking stride for the first time and then stopping, turning her head so she is facing Willard.

– My name is Orkul, she says, holding out her hand. Lia Ben-Orkul.

– I'm Willard, says Willard, extending his in return.

She shakes his hand and studies him, searches across his face. He stares back. Her hair is curled and falls thick down around her eyes. She juts out her bottom lip and tries to blow it clear, blows again, gives up.

– But I swear, she says, still holding his hand, the strangest thing. When the Elders dragged in Mr Elber's body, I'm sure his bindle was strapped to his back. And it looked full. Now why would he bring a full bindle to go hunting lizards?

A test? A sign? Willard has not the language to read it.

– He must have been bringing materials, Willard offers, for the nest.

– Yes, says the young woman, releasing him, for the nest, then. That must have been it.

And off she starts, leaving Willard behind.

RATIONS

It is not long after noon when Willard crests a small hill and sees a welcome sight in the distance – the red rectangle of a metal container.

It is sitting proud against the grey spurs of the mountains, a large and rusted oblong the colour of a dark broth. The container is nestled, as they always are when he finds them, in a crater as if it has been dropped from a great height. He asks Mother about this sometimes, but the answer is always the same: it's not important *who* gives the rations, only that they *do*. They have reached the end, found it to be bounteous – and they want us to get there too.

Willard drops the empty bindles and shields his eyes with his hand. He can make out people scurrying in and out of the container, preparing and distributing the allowances, little black dots drifting this way and that, crossing paths like the floaters sliding across his eyes. He knows that by nightfall all the supplies will be gone and then even the container itself will be broken down – to be used as wind-stops or for panelling or scavenged for nuts and bolts or anything that can be lathed or worked to form replacement phalanges and valves. Some people will even cut small squares from the metal, working through the thinnest parts of the steel with notched hacksaw blades until their hands blister. Hours and hours grinding metal to powder with a blunt saw, all so they might hang some paltry red square over a bed or behind a water basin – any attempt to add some patch of colour to the monochrome of their tarpaulin homes. And if the Line moves? Then it will be abandoned, too heavy to carry. But the act of scavenging is small humanity enough.

It takes Willard another hour to reach the container. The corrugated doors have already been unhinged and overlaid onto a line of five-gallon drums to form make-shift tables, and the provisions are set out on them in the allotted stipends, in neat and triangular piles. The man behind the first table is a little smaller than Willard, dark from the sun, thick in the forearms. His skin is karstic and red blossoms hang on his cheeks from the years of drinking whiskey. He is older than Willard, a little more worn, a little less interested, but otherwise not so different. He too has been carved out by a life of Lining Up.

– Name? he says.

– Willard B. Trophy.

The man checks a list with a deliberate precision and ticks off Willard's name.

– Bindle, he says.

Willard unslings his three bindles, buckles clattering as he drops them on the corrugated tabletop. The man looks at them and then back at Willard.

– One stipend per person, he says.

– I always collect three, says Willard, handing over Mother and Mr Hummel's signatures. They are too old; they can't make the walk.

The man stares at him, reads the names and then checks them against the list too. His face is not unfriendly, but his eyes are hard.

– You know the penalty for forgery?

– I know, says Willard.

– OK, he says, then disappears into the container. When he returns, he is carrying food enough for them all.

NYLA

Nyla is sitting inside her tarp on a battered rug, one of the few things her parents left her.

Three candles are dug into the bare earth around the rug and they spill their light into the tented room, catching and bending on the curvature of the pots hanging by their handles above the cooking stove. Around the stove are her boots and a small stack of tin mugs and plates. The top of a sack of pap is rolled closed, clamped shut with a peg and leaning indolent against the tarpaulin wall.

She has washed her hair and it is knotted like undergrowth about her shoulders. It took her an hour to first draw and then boil the water, but she carried the pail down the path of loose stones to the nearest water-vat because she knew it was a rations day – and Willard always calls on a rations day. He knows he is welcome anytime, but he likes to bring something. Nyla thinks he feels guilty because if they marry, when they marry, she will have to give up her place and move down the Line for him.

She is combing through the snarls of her hair with her fingers when Willard pushes open the plastic drapes, a brown package tucked under his right arm. He stoops inside, laying it down on the rug and then sits cross-legged before her. He looks but says nothing, as if he has come to worship before the altar of a small and thicket-haired votive inside a tarpaulin temple of all-will-be-fine. Nyla looks back at him through snow-holed eyes.

– You're late, she says, falling onto him with her arms open. Late, late, late.

– Am I so predictable? says Willard, grabbing her. They rock from side to side, the candlelight breaking on the knolls of their backs.

– Reliable, she says and kisses his cheek. Reliable.

That evening they feast. Willard has brought rich, dark coffee, brown bread and a wheel of veined cheese. He has brought a glass jar of dark-red jam made of spicy berries and covered by white muslin. He has brought long cuts of cured beef and a tin of olives steeped in oil; thick, white hummus that leaves a sheen on their fingers; smoky plums and brittle dryings of fish that snap in their hands. And he has brought his body, the trapeze of his shoulders, the strong line of muscle along his thigh, the smell of his fingers, and when they have finished eating they devour each other beneath the warping light of the candles, both becoming more stomach than mouth.

Willard dozes fitful, the fear of overstaying rippling beneath his lids, and he wakes to Nyla's head resting on his chest, the trickling light of the dying candle powdering her hair like a rust. The tent is still while, outside, all is the night.

– I had a dream, says Nyla. I was painting a sign. A young woman had offered me half of her rations to paint her a sign that she could hang outside her tarpaulin. I had never painted a sign before but I was so hungry.

Willard knows he should not speak. He imagines Nyla painting a sign and it makes him smile.

– She told me the sign was to say 'The Beginning And End', and then she left. But I had no brush and so I had to start painting with my finger, guessing at the size and width of the letters. I worked for days, not stopping for eating or drinking, until my hands had become only paint – but she did not come back. When I'd finished I sat by the sign, crying because I was so thirsty. Then I heard a voice and I looked up to see she had returned. She held out a cup of water but, when I went to take it, she poured it onto the dry earth in front of me and I watched each drop become a dusty ball. *This sign is wrong*, she said, *and I will not pay. But what's wrong?* I asked. *There is too big a gap between Beginning and And and And and End*, she said. *Too big a gap between Beginning and And and And and End, Beginning and And and And and End.* She kept repeating this until her words mangled together and all she was saying was *And* over and over again. I could see these three letters pouring endlessly out of her mouth.

Nyla is quiet and Willard squeezes her shoulder.

– That is it, Nyla says. Then I woke up. I wasn't even thirsty.

THE RUMOUR

The rumour blows down the Line like wind through long grass.

Willard and Mother are sitting at the fire drinking coffee when it comes. Mr Hummel, having finished his matins, is rolling his mat as usual with his white gown lit a ragged orange through the flames but then he does something they have never seen him do before.

Not in all their years.

He stops before his mat is fully rolled.

He cocks his head as if he has heard something creeping in the pre-dawn shadows, a noise grabbing him like some dark lasso, and he stands up, disappears into the murk leaving the mat behind. They wait for him to come back, with Mother wound so tight her hands turn pale from gripping her thighs. They sit, staring at his half-rolled mat. At last the wings of Mr Hummel's voice flap out of the gloom towards them.

– They say it is closed, that they are letting no more in. I don't know what to make of it but I thought you should know.

And with that Mr Hummel finishes rolling up his mat and disappears. Willard stares at Mother across the fire.

– What do we do? he says.

– Nothing, says Mother.

– But if it's closed?

– Everyone else is still Lining Up.

– What if they're wrong?

Mother sets her mug down in the dust.

– Stupidity and death have much in common, she says. Those affected never know, so it's the people closest to them who carry their burden. Tell me this, why have we Lined Up so long?

– To reach the front, says Willard.

– Exactly, says Mother. Yet you would have us leave and go to the back?

– I –

– You would have us betray our ancestors? Turn our backs on those who joined for us at the beginning, on all the others who held our places until we were ready to take them? Do you think the whole world has Lined

Up for nothing? That everyone is so wrong, so stupid, but that you alone are right?

– I don't know, says Willard, giving up.

– Then it's lucky I know. It's lucky I know we are here for something important. Unimaginably important. And if we leave now we will just rejoin later, and at the back. At the very back. Can you even imagine how far that is? How many places we would lose?

Willard can't. He takes a mouthful of his coffee.

– What if we didn't? he says.

– Didn't what?

– Rejoin.

Mother shakes her head and then shifts in her dirt-hollow to get comfortable.

– I always told you I never knew your father, and you always knew it was a lie. Well, here's your answer. And I promise you'll not like it, but since you persist with this silliness maybe it's time you heard. I did know him. And so did you, of a sort. He lived with us, here. In this tent, when you were still inside me. But he left us both. He left the Line.

The breeze picks up and a flapping sound starts, maybe the wind pulling at a tarpaulin or some flag being shaken or a leather belt doubled over and being snapped open and closed, something sharp and constant and elsewhere.

– No one's ever left.

– No, but your father did. It's a strange place we inhabit indeed. He was an apostate, Willard, and that is a fact.

Willard's breathing quickens, becomes shorter, more rapid, and in between the cracks of the flapping tarpskins he begins to hear the shallow janglings of his heart.

– The morning he left I woke up and I knew straightaway. The air felt different, not worse but different. And when I saw his bindle was gone there was no doubt. I tried to hide it. I told no one, when people began to ask for him I pretended he was lying sick in the tarp. I don't even know why. I knew I could never keep up the pretence, but I was young, heavily pregnant. And maybe I hoped he *was* lying sick somewhere, screaming in agony from the inside out. Of course, the Elders found out and I had to come clean. And not only had I not raised the alarm but now I'd lied. They burned all we had, everything, every grain of pap and scrap of cloth, and I should have then been stonehauled or had my tongue expunged – but Mr Hummel pleaded for me. *If not for her,* he said, *then for the child. Give her one thing and, if she manages to survive, then we know it's the Emperors who have willed it so.* So that's what they did, gave me a single square of tarp. And that's what I did too. Survive. Begged, borrowed … worse. But I survived. I was lucky; it was summer in the lowlands then. Otherwise those early nights would have finished me.

– That was it? The last you saw him?

– No. Two weeks later I was sleeping, wrapped in a sheet, and I was shaken awake by a ghost. He was starved, mad from dehydration, no more than a corpse. He was skeletal, almost naked, limbs so wasted that his head looked enlarged and his bulbous eyes shone out like mirrors from the grey ruins of his skin. *Please*, he whispered, *please. There is nothing out there, nothing. Take me back.*

– But you didn't.

– No. I didn't. He'd left me for dead – and you. And how could I anyway? The Elders would never have permitted it.

– And instead, you … did what?

– What I should have done the morning he fucking left. I went straight to Mr Hummel. The Elders caught him then alright, strung him up between two trees. They told the others he'd been found cutting in way up the Line and they'd brought him back to face justice. One by one we all cut the skin from his muscles. And I was the first to wield the blade. They didn't even need to ask.

Willard does not respond; his mind is aphids. He drinks his coffee in sips, shifting beneath the scrats of his shirt as the silence of the mites riot ravenous through his ears. His vision begins to swirl, greys and blues churning in the grainy pre-dawn dark, greens and violent pinks and purples like a thumb pressed into his eye and held there.

The wind drops and the flapping fades and Willard feels something stir. It is something that usually hides in him gnat-like, kept subdued by the ordered effort of the Line, but now it has been released. He feels it lurch, first just the twitching shadows from its spindle-limbs, but it crawls and claws up through him before emerging into his consciousness like a spider from an egg-sack, the viscera of Mr Hummel's words cascading from its every edge.

What if it is closed, it says, scuttling back and forth. *What if it is closed?*

Willard shifts his gaze to Mother across the fire. Through the vacillations of air her skin looks so worn and broken. It seems to him not skin at all, but rather the hide of some ancient lizard or the bark of a gnarled oak, as if someone has boiled down an ancient bone into char and used it to paint the concept of a face. *Look,* the rumour clatters in Willard's ear, *look at her. She is so hopeless, so extraneous and inane. What will she do now that it is closed?* It taunts him. *It is closed now and her life has been wasted. What is the point of her now?*

High up, a gyring hawk lets out a scree and the moment breaks.

Willard rubs his eyes and across the fire Mother is Mother once more and his love for her returns, falling back down upon him like a water drum. And looking up towards the hawk Willard sees that dawn is breaking.

And, with it, the rumour is breaking too. He sees it thrashing through its final throes as all its lying bowels are staked out across the purple clouds. Because right then it happens.

It finally happens.

It moves. It moves. It moves.

MOUNTAINS

It shifts and It shifts big.

It has been a long time since the Line has moved but Willard remembers it always starts in the same way. First comes the far-off rattling of packs and tarps, of tin mugs and plates being lifted as people rise up. Willard hears the noise hours before he sees any movement, a faint hissing to begin with, a rustling almost indistinguishable from the dust on the stones, but it hangs in the air, grows, thickens until the sound comes roaring down the Line, hurtles towards them, bursts over them in a fierce and oscillating crescendo – and is gone; fading away as the dopplering concertinas of its violence ripple away and disappear. Then, juddering into motion like the first turn in the shunting of some massive log, they stand and then start to walk.

It is impossible to say how any of these movements begin, who decides upon them or what is in charge;

whether they are the pull and push of some huge constant as the moon acting upon the tides or whether they are a more organised lunacy, the lustrous violence of a shoal of bait-fish or the unknowability of any individual starling superseded by the swaying certainty of the entire murmuration. But happen they do.

Clearing the foothills takes them almost two days. First comes a long and gentle rise, picking through tufts of knee-high bushes, but the coarse green of furze and broken brush then gives way to shin-length grass and Willard is guiding Mother through exposed roots and scrabbling over boulders. On the second day, the bushes and roots disappear and smaller clumps of flowers, boot-high with white and yellow heads, take their place. Then even the small flowers dissolve, leaving rocks; sharp and ankle-busting slabs of flint and shale.

Willard and Mother stop late the second afternoon and make camp, and soon after midnight they begin to climb again. And so the Line continues through the foothills, an uneasy rhythm falling upon It. Sometimes they move during the day and make camp at night, sometimes they sleep when it's bright and walk through the darkness, their silent steps lit by the gobbets of the moon.

They walk in shifts of eight, ten, twelve hours, and during each of these shifts they stop briefly and unpredictably, people hurrying to eat and drink and piss.

Willard and Mother continue towards the mountains in this erratic and sombre conga, climbing higher and higher along the narrow tracks. Shouts ring down to them from farther up the Line, warnings to avoid leg-snapping holes and pits in the track and, as they climb higher, the wind picks up and the temperature falls. People fumble to put on whatever extra coverings they have: quilted shirts, knitted jumpers that let the wind straight through, the lucky few with windbreakers. But still they keep climbing as they ascend the bluffs.

As they walk Willard looks down vertiginous cliff faces and sees the detritus that has been cast over the side by those in the places ahead; broken mugs, tent poles warped by the mountain winds or old pots with their bottoms burned through and all lining the floor of the valley far below, winking up like flakes of mica catching in the light.

But he sees other things too. Bodies. The splattered remains of people who have been unlucky enough to slip. Or the dried shells of the old and the infirm, those who stumbled too close to the edge and were first grabbed, then released: a kindness to spare them the walk through the high lands. Willard wonders how quick he will be to grab Mother if she strays too close to an edge – but he stops himself, shakes away the ugliness of the thought and takes her elbow, concentrating on helping her along the path.

Still the Line goes up and up. Still It keeps rising.

Is there anything less human than a mountain? Willard doesn't think so. He remembers the last time they crossed over a high pass. He was crippled by headaches as he struggled to adjust to the thinning air and the dry atmosphere ripped the lining from his throat, so he woke in the mornings coughing dust. His eyes reddened as the reduced pressure burst delicate capillaries and he was consigned behind the rocks, the contents of his stomach evacuated as his digestion shut down to divert oxygen back to his pulsing brain. What if this time we never come down, he wonders? What if this time we keep going up forever? How long before the mountains mould us all in their image? How long before they cut us all short and squat or their flaying winds slow-round our faces like they have the stones strewn across each empty slope?

But he guides Mother, helps her traverse the narrow path by making sure each foot is well anchored before she transfers her weight. The going is slow. Eyes down, he tells her, choose each step carefully, ignore what rolls down from above and instead concentrate on not displacing any herself. At least twice he hears someone lose their footing up the Line. He can't see what's happened but he knows any fall here will be painful.

They sleep twice on those narrow paths, wrapped in their unslung bindles and looking out at the leviathan truth of the Line below. There It is, stretching back for miles and miles, hundreds of thousands of bedraggled crabs carrying their homes on their backs, an impossible length that cuts through the heart of mountains and stretches back across the flat and soft lands behind. What if we never come out of the mountains? Better off lower down, to have summer on the plains; if the Line will keep moving surely It will keep moving surely surely surely and every day faceless faceless the same.

THE THIEF

It is three more days before they emerge from the mountains and the descent is better.

The wind dies off and the temperature rises, bare stones giving way once more to the clumps of white and yellow flowers; the occasional blooms at first, fighting through the rocks, but soon the grasses re-emerge and then the coarse bushes. The Line drops and the path steadies, becoming easier to walk on; the rocks are flatter, with soil packed between, and flanked by huge boulders as if a giant has flung them down from the peaks above. They hear birds again, the dull squawks of rock-dwelling hawks nested high in cliff faces. The path drops steep and hangs hard, picking up again the fast running stream, and brings them down towards the remains of a near-decimated tree line.

From a distance Willard can tell something is among the trees because he sees the hawks speckling the sky, holding above the trunks in blackening wait-wheels, and as the Line approaches a sound drifts up towards him, a dark noise soft and cruel as the easy flicking of a whip. But it is only entering the shabby thicket of broken boughs that he sees what is making the noise: a figure staked into an X between two trees, wrists and ankles lashed tight with white flex.

It is a man.

It was a man.

Not anymore.

Now he is a dripping red catastrophe. He has been de-skinned from his navel up, his head fallen forward onto his chest so Willard can make out the glistening of a domed skull, osseous white patches shining out where the scalp has been removed all the way to the bone. Stringy sinews and muscles are visible along the neck and arms, pink and wet, the few strips of skin that remain hide in the hollow pits of his clavicles. Willard sees a grey sheen where grit from the path has been rubbed into the patina of his body, sharp bits of sand and dust caking the weeping mass of the torso and over all this rough-shod filth the flies walk unhurried.

– Fuck, says Willard.

An Elder is standing beside the crook of the bend, a wizened woman gaunt as an empty pocket. Willard watches her hand something sharp to a young girl in the passing Line and point to the wretch strung up between the trees. The girl looks uncertain but, encouraged by her mother's gentle pats to the small of her back, she takes the knife from the Elder and shuffles towards the awful thing lashed between the boughs. She holds the blade by her side while she approaches, metal glinting against her thigh. The Elder follows behind. When she reaches the figure, the Elder takes her hand, tenderly, modelling how her tiny fingers should hold the blade, guiding her delicate hand to a tongue of soft skin below the man's seeping armpit.

The Line passes. The Line watches.

They watch the girl who, with growing confidence, strips off a length of skin and then picks a handful of dust from the floor. They watch the Elder show her how best to rub it into the mess of exposed tissue, teaching her to twist sharp the heel of her hand. A gurgling emanates from the splattered husk and Willard realises the thing is somehow still alive.

– Oh fuck, says Willard again. Oh please, oh fuck, oh fuck.

Mr Hummel hears, catches him by the wrist and pulls him out from the passing Line. He motions Willard's Mother to keep going and she shuffles dutifully on down the track.

– You know what this is? Mr Hummel says.

– Yes, says Willard. No.

– It's an Unplacing. The last was before you were born and then the man tied between the boughs was your father.

Willard hears a moan as if the wretch is breathing up through the bottom of a mug of coffee.

– I will not take the knife, says Willard.

Mr Hummel unslings his roving-pack, drops it heavy on the dirt and sits, pulling Willard down to join him. He fishes out a weathered bottle from the folds of his shirt and lifts it to his mouth. Willard watches his leathery throat bob as he drinks, then turns to see the Elder woman wiping the knife clean on her trouser leg, readying it for the next.

– What is a person who skips the Line? says Mr Hummel.

Willard sees Mother in what should have been Mr Hummel's place, nearing her turn to take the knife. He looks back at Mr Hummel, his grey hair being flicked by the wind and his sun-bitten eyes shaded by the brows jutting from his face.

– Don't worry, says Mr Hummel, I will take my turn when the moment calls for it. But answer me.

– I don't know, says Willard.

– They are a thief. Nothing more, nothing less. A thief. They steal your life from you, one second at a time. When they cut the Line they are really cutting *you*; they are saying that *your* time, the time *you* have waited, is not important; that *your life* is not so important as theirs, so they will take it from you because they've decided their life means more. When they skip the Line, every extra second they force you to wait cuts your skin away from your bones, sliver by sliver. And this is why we all must take our knives to him. Because he has already taken his to each and every one of us.

Mr Hummel holds out a sheath, the tan of the leather standing out against the pale skin of his palm. The sheath is about the length of his hand. It has a gentle curve so that the point rests over the gnarled tip of Mr Hummel's little finger and an ivory handle extends down the centre of his forearm. The handle is ornately worked, with ridges carved into the shape of fingers enclosing to a fist. The pommel is square and flat, and a screaming figure straddled into an X has been wrought in.

Willard ignores the knife and instead takes the bottle from Mr Hummel. He pours some water into his palm, rubs it first into his face and then onto the back of his neck and feels it trickle down between his shoulder blades. He hands back the bottle and takes the knife, turning it in his hands.

– He has done what he has done, says Willard. Nothing will be achieved by me taking this knife.

– Let me tell you a story, says Mr Hummel.

Willard continues to finger the knife.

– A long time ago, Mr Hummel says, before the Line, if you can imagine such a thing, if there ever was such a thing, maybe there lived a king. Or maybe a prince, if you'd rather, or a queen, or a sultan or a raj or a general or a despot. It makes no matter. A horrible monster ravaged the king's land for years. It was terrible indeed; half-man-half-bull maybe, or maybe a barnacle-encrusted kraken or some huge and poisonous ground-worm. But what matters is that the monster made any progress within the kingdom impossible – everyone existed in a perpetual state of squalor and fear. No sooner had someone managed to stop worrying about the monster and build something of worth than the monster would be sure to appear and wreck it, carrying them or their loved ones off into the forest – or the sea, or the cave or the mountains or back to the bottom of whatever dark lake from which it had emerged. But the king knew something. He knew that if he fed this monster – even once a year, maybe even just once every three or five – then it would leave them in peace. And all he had to do was feed it one single criminal, one measly thief or sordid murderer or rapist. And so that was what he did. And the kingdom blossomed. It flourished; it went from strength to strength. It has never looked back. So that is why you must take the knife,

Willard – because the Line is all we have. That is why you must take the knife, Willard. Because for us to continue what good we do, he must now suffer what he must. So that is why you must take the knife and why you must be seen to take the knife. Will you take it now?

Willard has unsheathed the knife as Mr Hummel talked and sees that, although the outer edges of the metal are in fact blunt, a long rectangular hole with sharp internal blades is scored down the middle. He sees that if the knife is held one hand on its curved tip and the other on the handle, it can be run down along a strip of skin, so sharp it will curl a thin ribbon of flesh back on itself, like a shaving of wood. Willard feels the air around him thicken, become febrile, as if it is sweating, and some green smell of sickness heaves down until he tilts his face up to breathe.

Mother is now on one knee, straining with both hands as she cuts a strip of skin from the thigh of the pulpy mess. Another damp moan and she returns to take her place in the Line, passing her knife to the first of the waiting Addison children.

No, not another child. Enough, enough. That is enough.

Willard stands without a word and strides towards the gurgling pile of slop, carrying the knife hanging down along his thigh as the child had done earlier.

THE MONSTER

Willard returns the blade and Mr Hummel pours a little water onto the bloodied metal before wiping it clean on his gown. Once it is sheathed, Willard extends his left fist to Mr Hummel and turns it closed-palm up. It is sticky with blood and gravel.

– How do I know he skipped the Line? says Willard.

– You know because he is strung up between two trees and you were cutting his skin off. But you shouldn't have killed him. You've taken that from the rest.

– Don't worry, says Willard. I punished him first.

He opens his outstretched fist.

On his smeared palm sit two narrow and bloodied strips of skin, the few remaining lashes giving them away as eyelids.

– Feed these to your monster, he says.

– Very good, says Mr Hummel. Very good.

THE TOWN

A few hours before it happens, the Line is still cycling through the biggest shift anyone can remember and, though they have descended from the high veldts, they are clearing the last of the slopes.

There are sporadic climbs and descents, but gentler now, and mostly they follow the petulant young stream that is starting to slow into a river. It is worse if they stop up on one of the plateaus – the wind has more teeth there – but, Willard thinks, at least he gets to see the campfires then, strung out across the plain for miles and miles.

They stop on a large stony level and Willard begins making camp for the night. Nyla, having dropped back to walk with them as she often does, is talking with Mother as they get the water on to boil. Willard has arranged the flimsy poles to protect their fire from the wind and is tying down the tarp as best he can. Every time he thinks he has a corner secured and is ready to make the final knot, the wind takes it and snaps it out of his hand, cracking like a stick. He listens to the women as he works.

– I suppose you expect me to say that it was better in the old days? That we had more and things cost less. That you children were better behaved? says Mother.

– Was it so?

– No. It has always been much as it is now. Some like to visit in the past, but they forget that even then we still all had to shit in the mornings.

A gust of wind blows in and the tarp whips up out of Willard's grip again. He swears as he scrabbles after the fluttering corner and brings it back under control, gets it tied using a double knot to lash the rusty eyehole hard against the thin wooden frame. Mother is still speaking.

– I passed through a town once. It was small and empty but the people ahead of us had left furniture and tools, even some beer fermented in glass bottles. We were stopped there for months, a year maybe, and people began to set up shops in the empty buildings. And a shower! It was made of pipes and a barrel and it ran on gravity somehow. The pipes passed through a stove and the water would come out scalding hot! We had a party. And in the mornings I would wash my hair under the steaming water and I was happy. It *was* better there. I could have stayed longer.

– Why did you leave?

– Why do we ever? The Line moved. We were sure we were close. Maybe that's what's at the end – a place like that.

– Do you think so?

– Who knows? But I hope it's not the sea.

Nyla must have looked at her open-eyed.

– You've never seen the sea, have you?

– No, says Nyla, it must be beautiful.

– It is. It was. We Lined Up by the sea once too. For weeks. The thundering waves hammering us to sleep, white lines rolling into the shore. And the birds – oh, the birds! It *was* beautiful, to begin with. But soon the salt began to eat at everything and the sand got everywhere and the wind never stopped blowing.

They fall silent and the wail of Mr Hummel's vespers drift in, landing down on Willard like some tale of sea spray landing on the dunes.

NYLA

After Willard finishes tying down the tarp they eat a quiet meal, of pap and dried fish mixed with starch-root, and when dinner is over he walks Nyla back up the Line. They pass the clinking of families clustered around flames and scraping the dregs of stew from their pots, groups of young men and women passing bottles around and laughing, old men singing as onlookers tap their feet and nod along attentively. The Line is moving; people are hopeful.

That night Nyla and Willard fuck, and for a few hours all is forgotten – the Line, the mountains, the never-ending cold – as all that matters seems hung upon their straining tongues. Outside Nyla's tent the wind shaking the plastic sheeting is constant but arrhythmic.

Nyla wakes sometime before midnight. In the darkness she can't tell if Willard's eyes are open or not but his breathing says he is awake.

– Your Mother said you talked of leaving?

– It's true.

– And you meant it?

– I think I did.

– But you did not talk of it with me?

– What would you have said?

– Maybe I would have said both my parents died in the Line so that I might not, so that I might reach the end. Maybe I would have said that I will not betray them, or the sacrifices of everyone who has gone before so that I might have this place.

Willard lets Nyla's voice scuttle over him. He reaches for his coiled disk of his jeans and feels his way to the pocket, takes out a hand-rolled cigarette which he lights with a cascading strike of a match. That is the problem, thinks Willard; in the Line the dead still have a say and their say counts for double. It's a necrocracy and so everyone left alive walks into tomorrow facing backwards.

– But maybe not, she says. Maybe I would have said I will go with you, that even though I know there's nothing out there I will still go with you to find out. But you didn't talk with me about leaving. So now you'll never know.

– I had a dream, Willard says as he smokes.

He speaks in a slow drawl, rolling each word in his mouth like a wingnut. But what he says is not true. He had not slept; he had lain awake, his mind clicking like a ratchet, each turn pulling him tighter and more wracked.

– A man had come to kill me, he continues, some bone-faced savage intent on my murder. For hours I fought him in my tent, thrashing against the canvas walls, like two dying fish in a bag. I tired; he cudgelled me flat.

He stops for a slow pull of his cigarette.

– I was injured beyond standing and he began to beat me where I lay, lashing me with whatever came to his hand – a pot, a chair, a poking iron for the fire. And on every beat he landed he spoke a word. *How-can-you-be-so-selfish?* he asked. *If you leave the Line we all suffer and how can you be so selfish?* At last he ran out of breath from the flaking he was giving me. *Speak*, he said, and I looked up, my face thick with blood. Then, from my cracked lips, came a question. *Tell me this,* I said. *If I stay in Line I suffer – but if I leave then the Line suffers. So why am I not part of the Line too?*

– What did he say? says Nyla.

– Nothing. He just laughed, laughed until his mouth grew so wide it swallowed us both.

Willard kisses Nyla goodbye and leaves to make it back to his tent and so not forfeit his place. And when he returns all has changed.

THE DISCOVERY

The fire is just a few embers marking angry patches against the dark when Willard reaches his tent.

Mr Hummel and Mother have long since turned in, and Willard sits by the fire staring into the suds of night. The rows of campfires along the plateau have all but disappeared, now just the occasional pinpricks of orange visible at intervals hard to judge. Willard sits and stares, throwing sticks on the glowing ash to ward off the cold. He checks he has left enough in the tinder-pile to get the fire going come the morning and then ducks in under the tarp.

There is a single candle still lighting, which has burned down to a stub, and at first inside the tarp seems blacker than the starlit night outside. However, once Willard's eyes adjust, he sees a shape in the middle of the earthen floor, heaped like the pile of sticks left by the fire.

It is Mother.

His pupils dilate in the gloom and he sees her right arm is trapped under her body at an unnatural angle, her left knee twisted so her foot points up and outward. It looks as if someone has let out her air, and she has crumpled down on herself. Willard attunes to her breathing, soft but frantic and tinged with fluid caught somewhere low in her gullet.

Willard has thought about this moment many times before. He is not morbid, but Mother has been frail for many years and the mountains have been unforgiving. However, in thinking about Mother's death Willard was always thinking about himself – despite his many imaginings and re-imaginings, every possible scenario conceived was viewed through the warping lens of himself. In those envisioned scenes, some ghost of his own eyes was forever hovering in the corner of the tent and recording the moment he would find her body, but it was his own actions that were being examined; how much he might cry or how enduring his pain or what eloquence he would utter at that moment of her passing, whether his loss would leap upon him like a fever or swallow him like a sink-hole.

Now the moment is here.

Now there is no ghost of himself hovering above to chronicle and weigh out stoic each gram of his grief;

instead he is alone, staring at the mangled thing that was Mother and hearing her life leaving her broken body in phlegm-bitten breaths.

And if grief has now come to him at all then it is dressed as something else – relief. Relief because this moment has come at last and so Willard no longer needs to worry about how he might act when he finds Mother's body – he has found it, and whatever he does now will be whatever he does and that will be all there is.

And what does Willard do?

He sits down. He slumps in the corner, leaning back into the wall of the tarp and feeling the night seep into him. He watches Mother, folded in a pile and lying almost still save for the faintest movement betraying her breathing. He watches and he shakes, shakes as he sees that time is water running through the purlins to put out her pitiful life. He shakes and he sits and he watches her die, until swords of morning slide through the tarp as if into a magician's box. And once she is dead – good and cold and dead – he gets up and tells Mr Hummel.

THE BOOK

Mr Hummel's gown crosses over and back above her buckled body. He mutters as his hands cut the air into symbols, figures-of-eight, ampersands, two dogs flattening out grass before sleep. *Letbebefinaleofseem* he mutters, *letbebefinaleofseem*.

– We must hurry, says Mr Hummel as he shuffles towards the doorway.

– Nyla, says Willard. She would want to be here. Mother would have liked it.

– There's no time, says Mr Hummel. We must hurry, I must prepare the body before the Line moves off and leaves us, and you must sort the possessions.

If there was any doubt that she was dead before, then there is none as Mr Hummel hefts up his soutane sleeves and grabs Willard's mother by the heels. He drags her across the floor with a surprising dignity, given that her arms trail after her, cutting pewter runnels through the dirt. He stops before the flap of the tent.

– It will be painful, says Mr Hummel. But you are one now, and whatever you decide to keep, you alone will carry. The rest you must leave. Remember that what seems lost to you will be a gladness to whoever stops here next.

– How long do I have? says Willard.

– One hour. Maybe a little more.

Mr Hummel leaves and Willard's mother trails after him.

Willard stands a long time before he starts sorting through the detritus of her life. He looks around at the meagre stacks of pots, the blankets, the bag from which the squids of Mother's clothes are inking across the dirt. This was the summary of her. All her life she had Lined Up and then died on the flattened plain of some unknown foothill, having never seen its end. Her paltry pile of possessions sits there in mockery like the scars of some botched operation.

First he picks up the two pots, crude receptacles that had been rough-hammered vaguely flat over the feeble flames of some tinker's fire. Originally each had a wooden handle, but the wood has long since snapped, leaving just rusted screw heads jutting out. He remembers how Mother had taught him to extend the life of the metal by dabbing a rag with a thin layer of oil and then wiping it over the inside after they had been washed. But so often the oil proved more valuable than the pot and instead they had been left to rust.

Willard decides to keep the least corroded one and leaves it to one side. He fires the other into the centre of the tarp, beginning the pile of things to leave behind. He holds the frying-pan in his hand to gauge the weight, trying to imagine how it will feel if added to his pack; experience tells him that what might not seem heavy in the hand slowly gathers weight when hiking, pulling down heavier and heavier step by step. He keeps it, along with a tin mug and bowl, throws the rest in in the middle of the earthen floor with the pot.

Next he sorts the food. He decides to leave the heavy sack of pap. The coffee he keeps, wrapping it tight in its paper packaging by folding the ends into triangles and then pushing them back in on themselves, mimicking the fastidious manner of Mother. The condensed milk he keeps too, sticky sided and rich, and a packet of dried fish, some dried fruit and a small bottle of whiskey. That is all; the rest he can scarcely carry. The tarp and poles he will keep, of course, and the water drum. And he decides too on the stoving chimney, it is light and stacks small enough to be wrapped in his bindle. It can always be jettisoned later if not needed.

Lastly, he turns to what he has been putting off: Mother's clothes, all of which had been stuffed into a large cotton shoulder bag, pulled half-shut by a double-knotted drawstring. Willard upends it, shaking it up and down so the clothes plunge out into a pile. Willard knows well enough the ten or twelve items Mother had owned and expects not to keep anything, but he gives them a cursory sift with a sweeping of his palms for anything forgotten or useful; a warm hat, or maybe something light and windproof. And that is when he comes across the dress.

At first, he thinks it just another of Mother's shapeless coveralls, loose fitting and roughly stitched. He lifts it, intending to cast it onto the centre pile – but he notices its weight. It is heavier than it has any right to be. He frees it out from the pile and holds it up by the shoulders, the hem hanging an inch clear of the ground. It does not fall evenly, sags in the middle. He balls it all up between his hands and squeezes around the stitching.

Substance. Resistance. Something inside.

He feeds the hem through his fingers – yes, there: a square about the size of his hand and sewn into the dress's pleated bottom section.

From his pocket he removes his knotted craft knife and, keeping one hand on the lump in the dress, opens out the blade with his free hand by levering it against his thigh. He tries to slice along the rough seams but the knife is blunt and notched from use, little better than tearing with his fingers. He changes tack, using the point to stab through the thinner material beside the hem and working down the fabric in a sawing motion, tearing more than cutting.

A few minutes and he has freed the object and discarded the dress – it is a thin book. It is different from the ornate leather-bound tome Willard has seen Mr Hummel read from at passing ceremonies. It is plain, simple, of no more than fifteen pages. It has a white cover with simple black lettering written across it, and its plainness seems a very bold statement.

It reads:

WELCOME TO THE CORPORATION
YOUR HANDBOOK

The pages are so stiff and sere, Willard has to prise each one loose by inserting a finger between it and the next. He turns through them but keeps half an eye on the door of the tarp – something tells him it will be better if he is not found reading it. What Willard finds written inside is simultaneously familiar and strange; although he can read each word on its own, when strung together they then appear alien to him. Although individually each word is translucent, the sentences they form become increasingly opaque.

But written in the bottom corner of the back cover is a sentence he does recognise.

And it is written in Mother's writing: *Ask for Ali Ben-Orkul.*

THE CEREMONY

Mr Hummel prepares the corpse by fixing the legs onto a high frame and then placing the head into a large earthen pot, which he has set on the ground. He nicks the throat and cooling blood seeps into the pot, steam rising off the warm surface in the curling patterns of some hand-daubed woad, and once the blood has been let he takes the pot and empties its fast congealing contents some distance from the tent before returning to de-joint the body. He saws through each limb with a rough-tempered blade, then wraps each dismembered section in a woven straw mat.

When the body has been fully dissected, Mr Hummel stacks it onto a plastic sheet – torso and head at the base, limbs on top – shaping a rough pyramid, pulling the corners together and tying a knot in the plastic. He runs a long wooden pole through and then calls Willard into his tent, instructing him to take the back. Once confident Willard is set, Mr Hummel grabs the front of the pole, swinging it out from his hip and up onto his shoulder with a bend of his legs, until the hoisted pole bows in the middle from the weight of the stacked corpse. And this is how Willard accompanies his mother on her final journey: stumbling through the half-light as he follows across the stony plateau.

Willard considers asking Mr Hummel about the book, but something stops him. A resigned silence has fallen and he concentrates instead on not losing his footing as, above him, the birds begin to circle. It takes them over an hour to get where they are going and the sky is shifting through ever-lighter shades of purple as the morning sun rises. Time is against them but Mr Hummel is relaxed; he knows going back will be quicker because they will not be carrying the remains, and they continue walking under a weight of hungry wings.

They reach a flat rock at the top of the ravine, looking out onto the width of the plain, and Mr Hummel at last seems satisfied. He stops, lowers his pole, and Willard too sets down his end of their macabre palanquin – and that is when he sees them all: twenty, thirty expectant beaks that have come to play their part in the passing ceremony of the sky burial.

– You might think this cruel, says Mr Hummel.

Willard's silence agrees.

– It's not cruel. Leaving her to rot on the plateau or be dug up by rock-foxes would be cruel, he says. This is kind; this is necessary, and Mr Hummel starts untying the plastic wrapping.

Willard fumbles to help but Mr Hummel motions for him to sit, and so Willard perches his chin on his knees and watches the birds. They are wide-spanned mountain vultures, carrion eaters with teal, finger-like wing tips and grey down on their necks. A few of the bravest of them have already landed and are hopping and squawking in fluttering leaps. Willard studies their hard beaks adorned with red and fleshy snoods, bright and lumpen like the inside of a pomegranate.

– The birds have their part to play, says Mr Hummel. The ground is too hard for a burial up here, we could not get more than a foot down. And wood is too valuable to build a pyre.

Mr Hummel takes out the smallest of the straw packages from the plastic and unwraps it. Despite his earlier letting, blood has soaked through the straw in blotches and Willard watches as Mr Hummel removes Mother's hands and flings them out one at a time into the feathery mass. A raucous shrieking goes up as the birds tear at the flesh, pulling each hand between three or four snapping beaks until the fingers pop off at the joints and the victors retreat to pick over their gristle-bones in solitude. More and more birds whirl down with piteous cries, kicking and pecking their way through the roil, and into this effervescent and fluttering mass Mr Hummel continues to throw Willard's Mother: her feet, her shins and forearms, her thighs. Soon all before them is a spume of feathers.

As Mr Hummel reaches for her head, Willard buries his face into his lap – but Mr Hummel grabs the back of his neck, squeezing below the ears with middle finger and thumb until the pain forces Willard to lift his eyes.

– Look. You must look, he says. Death should not be welcomed, but it should never be feared. She has died so that you may see the end. Died for you – never forget it. *Let be be finale of seem.*

And with that he lifts her naked head with two hands and bowls it underarm into the squall of birds.

LEAVING

Willard waits until Nyla's breathing slows, her chest rising and falling like the gentle pumping of a blacksmith's bellows, and untangles himself by lifting her leaden arm and sliding out from under it. He dresses quietly and grabs his pack. Then, taking a deep breath, he does what the Elders deny anyone else has ever done – he leaves the Line.

He exits the tarp and walks through the dark, picking uncertain footsteps through the rocks, his falling soles clacking on the stones like bones stripped of cartilage. He walks, the Line at his back, until out of the dark he hears the voice he has been expecting.

– I will not stop you.

Mr Hummel is alone, sitting on a rock and drinking from a bottle and Willard smells the oily whiskey. He bids Willard over with a patting of his hand.

– There is nothing out there. But if you won't take my word for it then I'll not stop you.

Willard sits down beside him.

– Nothing? he says.

– Nothing.

– Not even rock-bears?

– Come, say Mr Hummel. Put away your childish things.

– So, we don't believe in rock-bears anymore, he says. Just in flaying people alive.

Willard shifts on the stone to dispel the cold already seeping into his legs.

– Belief? Mr Hummel says, his voice gathering flint. Let me tell you about belief. Belief is what puts food in your belly, what keeps the rations coming. Belief is what gets people up in the morning and then what stops them murdering each other to try grab a better place in the Line. It's more belief that we need, not less of it. And believe this: There is nothing left out there.

– How do you know? says Willard.

– Because we are all here! Why would we endure It if there was really anything else?

Mr Hummel drinks from his bottle, then pushes it into Willard's hand. He feels the glass, warm from Mr Hummel's grip.

– You know your mistake? says Mr Hummel.

– Yes, says Willard. I dare hope for better.

– Hope? says Mr Hummel. No, hope is normal. We all hope. But you? You *expect*. *That's* the mistake. Ben-Orkul is nothing but a myth – a fable, a seed of dissent sowed when someone is jealous their neighbour has been deigned an Elder instead of them. Let me guess, you first heard the name from a pretty girl who you met in passing? What was it this time – Lia? Ila? That's how they work, Willard, the apostates. That's how they make you think you know something when in fact you know nothing at all. They want to trick you, to tempt you to leave, because they know that, if you do, sooner or later you'll come crawling back – and then they'll be the first to take the skin from your bones. Because each time they succeed there's one less person in front of them and they are one place closer to the front.

Willard drinks the whiskey and feels it burn down his oesophagus. He shifts the bottle, grabbing it between his knees, then coughs into both hands until the burning passes. He drinks again and this time he is ready for what comes, but still can't stop himself from coughing.

– I won't be back, he says.

– You will, says Mr Hummel. I've watched them all come back. Every single one. They all come scuttling back in the end, just like your father did.

Mr Hummel gets up, fixes to leave.

– You'll discover this for yourself, of course. And, when you realise you're out there alone, so terribly wrong and alone, you'll come back too. And maybe I'll let you back, Willard, concoct some story and move you far off down the Line. Or maybe I won't, and we'll take the skin from your body. But keep the whiskey, he says. You'll need it.

And with that Mr Hummel disappears into the night.

Willard stiffens, clenches his hands hard around the curves of the bottle. He sits and drinks for a long time, his back to the Line lest the sight of It melt the waxen seal of his resolve. He sits and drinks until the bottle is empty and then sits some more.

Three times he thinks he hears the rustle he's been waiting for – and three times his heart cracks when he realises it is the wind carrying grit across the stones. The fourth time he hears it, a soft scratch-scratching on the track below, he does not let himself believe. He sits there frozen, his eyes welded closed – until Nyla's arms land around his shoulders.

– You came, Willard says.

– You thought I wouldn't?

– I knew you would try ... but I was afraid –

– Don't say it, Nyla says. Don't say it, I'm here and don't ever say it.

– Are you ready? says Willard.

– Yes, says Nyla.

– Are you sure?

– Are you?

– I was, says Willard. But I found something.

He reaches into a clandestine flap he has sewn into the lid of his bindle and pulls out the book. Hands it to Nyla.

– It was hidden in the hem of one of Mother's dresses, he says.

She takes it from him and, like Willard had done earlier, prises the pages open.

– What is it? she says.

– I don't know, says Willard. I read it but it made no sense. Something about the Corporation.

– A group? Of Elders?

– No, I don't think so. Something else. And a place called Nodnol. And there is a man: Ali Ben-Orkul. But I couldn't work it out.

– I think it's important, says Nyla.

– I think it's dangerous, say Willard. It's not too late. We can still go back.

– No, says Nyla. No going back.

Willard pauses, thinking of Mr Hummel's final words.

– OK, he says. No going back.

They get up and walk together, both imagining the lights of the Line dwindling behind them. They walk and keep walking until, come the morning, they enter the great and ochre vault of the empty plain and start to trek across its vastness. They see nothing there, nothing but the dust kicking up from their shamble-gait feet. And they hear nothing either, save the clanking of the scabbed pots tethered to the outside of their roving-packs or the blood-thump in their ears over the guttural moans of the wind.

By mid-morning their hunger makes them stop and they sit on their bindles, drinking sparingly from their canteens and sharing out a scroggin of nuts and raisins from a small pocket-bag. Then they get up again and, squinting out from scraps of cloth wrapped around their faces to stop the grit grazing their corneas, they start to walk once more, leaving the Line far far behind.

II

TREKKING

Willard and Nyla are slumped on their packs somewhere in the vast and sepulchral plain.

They have realised that, deep down, they always knew there was nothing out beyond the Line. And they have realised too that neither ever knew what nothing truly was. Not until now.

But now they know it is this: no sound save the wind's constant keening, dust and stones, not a bush, not a bough, not a blade of grass, not so much as a cloud for shade nor fabric enough to make a hat to hide them, the sun so serrated it cuts through their clothes and then a night like stone, so they wish the sun back to scour them raw, their food nearly eaten, their water all gone, so tongues grow like gorse in their mouths.

And silence. A silence between each step saying *we're dead and we're dead and we're dead but I loved you.*

Nyla is asleep so it is Willard who first sees the men approaching. He sees them from a long way off, so far he can't be sure he's seen them at all, but the two scuttle-bugging specks begin to grow larger against the frozen horizon. He watches, squinting, sees them get bigger and bigger until he can make them out approaching with their chins sunk into their tasselled jackets. He calls to Nyla, who opens her eyes but stays lying listless on her pack. Willard and Nyla watch them approach, no one speaking, until the men draw up to them and stop. One man is large; the other smaller, angular and crimped, and it is the angular one who breaks his vigil.

– It's selfish of you to try and skip the Line, he says, looking at Willard. Now you must come with us.

– We're not skipping, Willard says, shading his eyes. We've left. For good.

The angular man tilts his head to his companion and the large man steps forward, striking Willard below the ear with the butt of his hand. The strike is lazy but controlled, thrown from his hip and so has his whole weight behind it. It comes from an angle outside Willard's vision and the first he knows of the crashing blow is the petals of a white flower-head unfurling behind his eyes. He's knocked to the ground, his ears flood full of ringing.

Nyla is up now – but before she can react the large man pinches Willard by the Adam's apple and forces him hard to his feet. He stumbles, then clatters into Nyla, who is sent sprawling on her back and the angular man pins her down with his boot.

– No one leaves for good, he says, staring down at her.

Nyla can see the boot is good quality. It has excellent stitching and a thick sole with wide and diagonal treads. She can see what is wedged between them: mud and sand and sharp stones.

– *We* did, she says between breaths.

His eyes flick over.

– No, you didn't, he says and presses down on her throat.

Nyla can't help but groan as the little air she has left is squeezed out and her back bites against the stones. He slides the toe of his boot up to her chin and forces her face around until she is looking at the large man, still holding Willard by the neck.

– You didn't leave, he says to her. You're skipping. And when you skip you are stealing – from me, from him, from our children. You would steal our lives to add them to your own. But now you will come with us.

The angular man motions to his companion again. This time, and with a surprising speed, the large man swings a knee at Willard, catching him inside the pelvis. The force makes Willard's head come forward and it meets the large man's upper-cutting fist, cracking Willard right where his septum meets his lip. He is knocked flat once more, this time his skull catching with a thud on the sharp-edged shale. He feels a front tooth loosen and his eyes fill with water. Something warm gathers on the back of his head.

– You're selfish little shits, the large man says.

He throws back a leg and then sinks a toecap into Willard's rib cage, the weight of the boot making his foot swing pendulously before hitting Willard's side with a noise like a wooden stave sounding out a cavity.

– You skipped the fucking Line, he says.

Six more weighted digs into Willard's ribs.

– You. Fuck. Ing. Skipped. The. Line.

Still Willard and Nyla stay silent.

– Fine you fucks, have it fucking your way.

The large man raises a foot and holds it high above Willard's face. It hovers there so Willard can gauge the full weight of what is going to come down on him: the tread, the mud and stones, the heft of the man behind.

THE CONFESSION

It is Willard who breaks.

– We skipped, he blurts from between the protective covering of his arms. We skipped, we skipped, we skipped.

The angular man now nods a third time and his companion lowers his foot. He takes a step backwards and Willard is left sprawled on the rocks, nursing his ribs and testing the anchorings of his teeth between an index knuckle and the pad of his thumb.

The angular man removes his own boot from Nyla, motions her to stand, and once she is on her feet, unbuttons his jacket and reaches inside. Against the quilted grey lining she sees the black sheath of a knife and for one terrible moment waits for the blade to emerge – but his hand comes out holding a water bag. He untwists the cap, the sinews of his forearm rippling under his skin, and lifts it to his mouth with both hands. He takes a long draught and, once finished, offers the bag to Nyla.

Nyla hesitates, expecting the worst – but the angular man continues to stand with the bag on offer and she snatches at it before he can rescind. She throws the spout to her mouth and water bubbles out her nose, spills over her cheeks and neck. She runs out of air, stops, coughs, then falls to drinking again – but this time, not fearing the bag being snatched away, is more measured. When she is finished the angular man takes back the bag and now hands it out to Willard. He winces as he sits up to take it and, despite the blood coming from his swollen lips, goes about his drinking much the same.

– How did you find us? says Willard, panting as he hands back the almost empty bag.

– Don't mistake us for stupid because we gave you something to drink, the large man says.

He points in the direction from which the two men came.

– The Line's just over there. We saw your buckles glinting from the watch-post. Now you're coming with us and, tomorrow, when the Warden decides it, we will take your skin off your body. Strip by fucking strip.

The large man gives Nyla a vicious shove in the back to get her moving and Willard, knowing he has no choice, stands up and follows on behind.

FLINT

When Nyla wakes up she finds herself lying in the corner of the earthen floor, her hands trussed tight behind her back.

The angular man had been right somehow. The Line had been close, less than a day's hard hike from where they were picked up, but yet not a section of the Line Willard or Nyla had ever seen before. They were route-marched flat across the high plain and, on reaching the perimeter, were handed over to a group of waiting Elders who immediately drowned Willard and Nyla under a flood of denuding hands. The Elders had said nothing as they ripped away Willard and Nyla's packs, had kept their mouths shut tight and silent, but their eyes they let speak – and their eyes spoke of violence. Then, with packs gone, they lashed Nyla's wrists and shoved her into a tarp wherein, despite what was hanging over her, exhaustion brought down a deep and barren sleep.

Now she is in a small holding-tent. It is scarce big enough that she can stand without touching the roof, and totally bare save the insects walking unworried along the canvas seams. It's morning and the air in the tent is already stale and, as the sun rises higher, the heat continues to beat down until it becomes ever more cloistered and breathless.

Nyla wishes she still had her pack. She knows that inside, tucked deep into the top flap, is the single piece of flint she readied before she left; the one she spent hours rubbing against a metal bowl and then testing with her thumb until she was sure it would draw blood. She has seen what they do to those who are accused of skipping. And she promised herself she would take that flint to her own neck before she'd let them do it to her. Or make Willard do it to her. Or worse, her to Willard.

But now her pack is gone and her hands are bound. The heat turns her fetid as the day wears on, making her sweat even just lying still on the floor and she spends her time not planning escape but simply wishing for water.

The hours pass. The sun blazes. Heat draws down her throat with every breath.

THE WARDEN

Nyla doesn't know how long she's been waiting when the swishing of a canvas flap finally announces the Warden's arrival.

The Warden enters holding a wooden crate in her hand, which she sets in the middle of the tent with a loud thump, and then sits upon it. Nyla, with an effort, sits up and studies her. She is tall and bland, not attractive or unattractive, carrying an air of something avian. For a long while the Warden says nothing, knowing how to let time cock its hammer, and when she does speak her voice is low, carrying a singularity of purpose.

– You skipped the Line, the Warden says, but adds nothing more.

Nyla had always thought she could read something behind the mask people presented her; that they liked singing or gathering stones or cared to drink early in the mornings, that they loved their children or hated their parents. But with the Warden there is none of this, no veneer hiding something underneath. The Warden's face is clear, unambiguous. It's a face carved out by seeing other people's suffering as a necessity; a face that realised, and early on, that violence came easier than scrapping in the detritus with everyone else. It's a face that found, long ago, that its most valuable currency was cruelty – and now it intends to spend it.

– No, says Nyla. We left.

– No one leaves, the Warden says, her expression still unflinching.

– We did, says Nyla.

– You skipped. You admitted it. Now you must pay.

A simple sadist would be better, thinks Nyla. With a sadist you might hope to turn them on something else, something that might squeal louder than you. But there is no hope of distracting the Warden. It's clear she is inexorable; that the Warden knows in an impoverished world her greatest asset is her blandness of character, a blandness that commits her to be in every respect a Warden and in no respect anything else. She is the Warden first and the Warden last and she will prove it here by cutting the skin from Nyla's bones.

But maybe there is one chance.

Nyla's mouth is dry. She swallows, forces herself to continue.

– You're right, says Nyla. We didn't leave.

– Good, says the Warden. She stands, knees bent to avoid the tarp roof hanging low above her, and sidles around until she stops half-stooped over Nyla's shoulders. Nyla feels a tug, then a sawing and at last a pinging-snip as the Warden cuts her arms free: a final disingenuous benevolence.

– Good, she says. See? It's better to be honest. Your boyfriend would soon have confessed in any case.

There, thinks Nyla as she rubs at the reddened welts on her wrists. There, what she wanted. They've not interrogated Willard yet, there may still be hope. Nyla's heart pounds so hard her chest trembles through her shirt; the Warden smiles her smile.

– We didn't leave, Nyla says. We were sent. To find you.

– And who was it that sent you? Says the Warden. What was so urgent that they couldn't come themselves?

Nyla concentrates, slows her breathing right down by drawing air in through her nose and then pushing it out through her mouth. When her shaking is contained, she takes one more breath and speaks.

– It was Ali Ben-Orkul.

THE NAME

The wind of this name blows a ripple across the Warden's face. For a moment her countenance cracks – eyes widen a fraction, lips uncurl – then it sets and hard as ever. But it's enough. Enough for Nyla to know her gambit has worked.

– And did Ali Ben-Orkul give you anything? the Warden says. Or did you perhaps lose it along the way?

– Yes, says Nyla. He gave us the Handbook. It's stitched into the lid of one of the bindles.

The Warden puts the index finger and thumb of her right hand in her mouth and lets off an ear-piercing whistle. The angular man from the plains comes in, ducking through the tent door, and the Warden ushers him over and whispers in his ear, the sound of skittering leaves. He nods, then disappears.

– For your sake I hope that is true.

The Warden stays seated. Nyla waits. All is silence, all is time.

When the angular man returns he is holding the book. He gives it to the Warden, then disappears again.

– I will say this once, says the Warden, turning the pages as she speaks. When I leave this tent, you are going to wait ten minutes. Then you are going to walk outside where your things will be waiting. You and your boyfriend will have the rest of the day to trade for whatever water and food you need and by evening you must be gone. You will first walk west for two hours, to beyond the perimeter, and then you will follow the Line along –

– Along? says Nyla.

– Along, confirms the Warden.

She pauses and, taking a piece of lacquered charcoal from her breast pocket, makes a series of intricate symbols on every page. She holds up the pages for Nyla to see.

– If anyone stops you, she says, show them my signature and you will be safe. Follow the Line for five days, maybe six; first north, then turning north by north-east until you reach a river. Track the river downstream, away from the Line, and somewhere there, if you have been quick enough and listening enough, you will find it.

– What?

– One of two things, says the Warden. Either the thing that will be waiting for you. Or else a great and grey-curtained emptiness, which will swallow you up without a sound.

With this, the Warden gives the book back to Nyla and leaves the tent, taking the crate with her.

TREKKING

The trek to the river is long and featureless and at every step the strangeness of their new journey rattles in them like a broken spoke.

They keep the Line to their right, over the horizon. They are careful not to stray too close to the latrine pits running along the outermost perimeter, so they track It during the day by the rising smoke and by night they watch the faint orange glow of Its fires catching on the underbelly of the clouds. The land is flat here, and there is grass as they walk, clumps and tufts, sometimes even occasional bushes and flowers. But mostly it is wind and stones.

They had hoped to be moving more quickly, had wanted to push on further between rests, but they are carrying six days of provisions. The food is heavy enough but worse are the water-bags, twenty litres strapped on to each of their packs so that the full bags swing back and forth with the rise and fall of their steps, a pendulous motion that constantly shifts their centre of balance and sucks the strength from their legs as they fight to keep their equilibrium. They hate the water but can think only of it. They've already broken their rationing.

And if they don't reach the river in time?

Then they know from their time in the high plains what will await them.

THE SECRET

It's late on the second afternoon when they stop for a meagre meal of cold rice and dried fish. They eat it greedily from small pouches, both haunched on their bindles, share a water bag and once finished they stand and continue to trek.

– I don't understand, says Willard as he walks. Mother had the Handbook, had written Ben-Orkul's name on it. She must have known *something*. So where did she get it? And why did she keep waiting?

Nyla stops walking.

– We hid the book, she says, only showed it when we had no other choice. Maybe she had no more clue than us, thought it was dangerous too?

Willard is so lost in himself it doesn't register, lets a big gap open up before realising he is alone. He stops and turns around.

– But how could she stay? he shouts, his voice cracking.

Nyla crosses the stony pits of earth and puts a hand on Willard's shoulder.

– And what should she have done? Gone? Left you behind? Deserted you forever for a name in a book she probably didn't understand?

– She should have told me.

– Told you what? That your whole life, everything she ever believed and told you to believe might be a lie? Would you have listened? Did you listen to her and Mr Hummel when they tried explaining other things to you?

Willard wilts at the knees, sags downwards.

– No, he says.

– No, says Nyla. And neither did I.

– But she should have told me … something. Told someone.

– And what if you'd let it slip? Or a troublemaker overheard? She could have been skinned before the words left her mouth. You judge her too harshly. She'd spent her whole life believing. Her whole life being certain. Then to throw that all away on a suspicion? That you, her, her parents, might have been wrong somehow? How could anyone do that to themselves? To their child? Most people just need a reason to get up in the morning, even if it's a bad one. Your mother was no different.

– You would have told me, says Willard.

– Would I? Some things survive so long they grow too big to fail. Then it's easier for everyone to stay quiet, to pretend no one knows.

Nyla pauses, takes her bottom lip between her teeth.

– But there is *something* I haven't told you, she says.

– What? says Willard.

Her voice emerges like a tin-lid, gouges a rent in the still air between them.

– I'm pregnant. I've missed three periods and my breasts are sore. I'm feeling sick and tired in the afternoons.

Willard feels his skin flush, a rising in his stomach. For a moment he wants to admonish her – to shout and scream and fling his bindle down on the earth – but he knows too well why she has waited. The heat leaves him.

– Then we shouldn't have come, he says sitting down in the dirt. We shouldn't have started all this. There's nothing out here. There never was.

Nyla steps forward, kneels down and puts an arm over his neck, pulls him in towards her.

– You think we should have stayed? she says into his ear.

– Yes.

She strokes his cheek with the back of her finger.

– No. I don't fucking know. But how can we bring a child up out here?

– How can we not? she says. How can we sacrifice one more body to such a senselessness of waiting? Have you already forgiven your mother for doing it to you?

– But there's nothing out here, says Willard.

– There is, says Nyla. We're out here.

– There's nothing out here, says Willard.

– There is, says Nyla. There's a river. And something waiting beyond it.

– Or nothing.

– Or nothing, she says and her voice growing strangely buoyant. But even if it's nothing then there will still be something.

– How? says Willard.

– My love for you, says Nyla. What else do you need?

THE DISCOVERY

On the evening of the fourth day Willard and Nyla are about to make camp.

They are sitting together on a large flat rock and the Line is hidden by the horizon, but they can see smoke rising in places, sometimes in clouds and sometimes in narrow and twisting trails like ropes dropping from the sky.

Nyla is unswagging her bindle and Willard sits with his legs dangling over the edge of the rock, ciphering in the dirt with a stick.

– What have you noticed since we left the Warden? he says.

– Stones? says Nyla. Blisters?

– No, says Willard. About the sun?

Nyla pulls out her sleep sack and starts to unroll it.

– That it's hot? she says.

– That it's moving, says Willard.

Nyla laughs.

– Of course it's moving, it moves all day.

Willard sits up, becomes animated.

– No, where it *rises* is changing; it's changed since we started walking.

– So … says Nyla.

– So why would that happen if we are walking in a straight line? Look – what way did we walk when we first left?

Nyla thinks for a moment, scratching her arm with a nail.

– East, she says.

– Exactly, says Willard, it was east. We walked directly away from the Line and kept the sun on our face in the mornings. So, we were here. He marks a point in the dirt with the stick.

– And we walked east for three days. He draws an arrow away from the point.

– And, when we left, the Line was running from south to north. He draws another arrow, this time perpendicular.

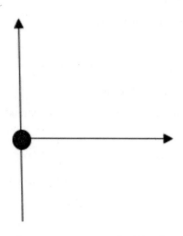

– But, when we were marched back, it was only a day's hike. We were marched hard, but we never covered three day's worth of walking. What way was the sun then?

Nyla thinks again.

– It was setting to the left of our faces. So we marched … north-west?

– Exactly, says Willard, and he adds another arrow.

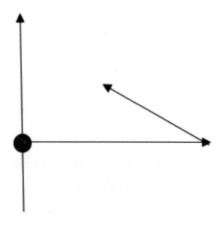

– So what happened? he says. Did the Line turn?

– It could have, says Nyla. It turned in the mountains sometimes. Or maybe it met a river?

– No. We were out of the mountains. And if it was a river, we would have seen it. The Warden told us follow the Line north then north by north-east. Willard adds another series of arrows:

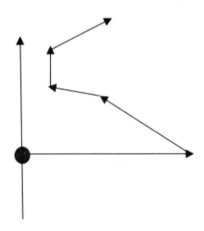

– But if the Line was turning sharply all the time we'd have seen it turn before, or now that we've left we should keep crossing over and back into it. The Warden said follow it *along* – you're sure she said *along*?

–Yes, says Nyla. She said it twice.

– Well then, here's what I think, says Willard. The Line didn't turn *at a right angle*. It couldn't, because It wasn't running straight. And It never has been. *Along,* the Warden said. Follow It *along.* But she didn't mean along *a straight line*, she meant along *an arc*. The Line's not straight – it's curved. And it's always been curved, all the time we've been in it, but so gently that we never noticed.

He draws another shape in the dirt.

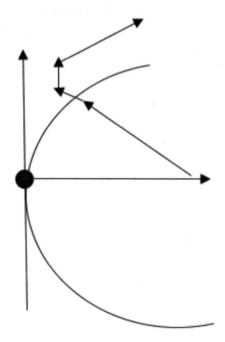

It takes a moment for the full weight of this to break on Nyla but once it does she sits up. Her head is bent forward, two fingers pressing to her temple.

– If it's always been curving, then the bend must be … huge … and if it keeps on curving –

– and if it keeps on curving, says Willard, making one final shape in the dirt, It will end up back where It started.

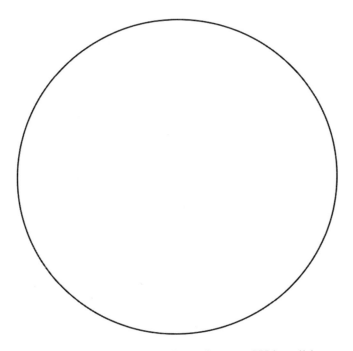

– There's no end of the Line, he says. We've all been waiting for nothing.

THE THING

They reach the river after two more days, just as the Warden predicted. It is wide and slow-moving, not like the little stream they had followed in the mountains. It is old water, old and tired, and it seems to say to them the sea is close.

Willard is tired and Nyla has been losing more and more sleep, getting up to piss throughout the night. Willard has seen her energy start to slump, watched her try to suck in her breath and rub the hot prickles away from her afternoon skin. They have spent days trying to encourage each other by talking of how much better their trek will become once they reach the river. They know then they will be able to walk unencumbered by water bags, stopping instead to fill up when needed. They know then that they will no longer need to wash their pots in a teaspoon of water, will be able to drink freely, boil rice, have coffee, bathe each morning or evening – both if the mood should take them – that they will still have food left, that the sun will be warm and the land will be flat. And although all these things prove true, the trek becomes no more pleasant.

They follow and follow the river and, for all that the trek is now easier on their legs, their physical exhaustion gives way to another type as they take to carrying a weight as heavy as the loaded water bag – but more insidious because it can't be halved or shared out or swapped between them when someone is flagging. It is a heaviness that each of them must carry by themselves. Reaching the river slakes their throats but it causes their minds to wither; their thoughts start to crack and warp under the unrelenting ingress of the roots of that single question: *but what if it's not even there?*

Neither Willard nor Nyla have any idea how far they should walk. Neither knows what they are looking for – what it is or where it might be, if it is still waiting or if they have missed it. They don't know even how they can *know* if they've missed it. The anxiety grows inside with each step until it is all either of them can think about. It drinks all conversation; they keep silent because they cannot keep asking each other for assurances neither of them can give.

But just when they are convinced they've lost whatever they might be looking for, can take it no more, are thinking of throwing their packs into the river and themselves along afterwards, they see it in the distance, tethered to a flat open stretch of riverbank. It is about the size of one of the cargo containers the rations arrived in and they both know that this is the thing that is waiting.

– That's it, shouts Willard and jumps into the air.

– That's it, says Nyla. That's it that's it that has to be it.

They take off running, their packs jingling in excitement as they make their way down the riverside.

Willard remembers how the Elders had once helped people board a boat when the Line had to cross a river and, getting closer, they see the thing waiting for them now is similar – but it is metallic, not wooden, and it is much, much larger. It is bobbing on the water with a narrow plank running between the deck and riverbank. The plank has a wooden handrail on one side and standing by the foot of the plank is a man. He waves at them from a distance and keeps waving until they reach him.

– Willard and Nyla? he says.

– Yes, they say, out of breath from their exertion.

He is tall and is wearing a uniform of some description, dark cap and dark trousers with a white shirt. He is holding a clipboard and greets them officiously. His voice is hollow; it rattles out of him like rice shaking in a bottle.

– I was about to leave, he says. But, before we continue, I must ask you some security questions.

He turns a page on his clipboard.

– Name of your Elder?

– Elder? says Willard.

– Yes, says the Captain. The Elder in charge of your Arc?

– You mean … Mr Hummel? says Nyla.

– Very good, says the Captain, making a tick on his paper.

Now they've had time to study him, Willard sees the Captain is odd in the extreme, a real peculiar. He is thin and his face seems empty behind the eyes, a vacancy that gives Willard the impression that, could he somehow open him up, he would deflate on the spot, crushed flat as the emptiness inside him mixed with anything having even a hint of substance.

– And who recommended you? the Captain says.

– Recommended us? says Nyla.

– For what? says Willard.

– For this, says the Captain.

– Who sent us? says Nyla.

– That will do.

– The Warden, they both say together.

– Very good, says the Captain and makes another tick on the paper. Last one. What Arc are you from?

Willard and Nyla look at him blankly. This one they can't even guess.

– Forty-degrees twenty-minutes maybe? No? What about this?

He turns his piece of paper around to show them. On it is a large circle covered with indecipherable scribblings and their faces grow more confused.

– Ring any bells?

Willard takes the picture from the Captain and holds it close up to his face.

– What *is* this? he says.

– You don't know?

– I do, says Nyla.

– Well? says the Captain, raising an eyebrow.

– It's the Line, isn't it?

– Very good, says the Captain. And not to worry, no one ever knows their Arc; I don't know why they insist on us asking that one. But I'm sure you're the right people. Come on board.

They follow him up the plank and they find themselves standing on a small wooden deck. It is surrounded by railings and, with the exception of an enclosed room in its centre, is uncovered. There are benches running up and down either side with seats that look like they can be tilted up so things can be stored in the base. There is a small silver chimney pipe near the hindmost railings and, beside it, a door that seems to lead down below deck. Folded and stacked neatly near the front railings are two sets of dark woollen blankets.

– You will be sleeping here, says the Captain, pointing to the blankets. I will be sleeping in the bridge, he says pointing to the room, which is strictly off-limits for you, as is the door to the engine room. If you need water, please ask, but all food is at your own expense. That's the tour done so let's get going.

– Where? says Willard.

– Where? says the Captain, his voice rising an octave. Where? Are you *sure* you've read the Handbook?

He consults his clipboard.

– It definitely says that you've received one. It's not often I have to sail with just two, but they were impressed that you'd already read it; they think you'll be quicker to get up to speed. Have you actually got a Handbook? If not, I'll have to insist you wait for the next sailing.

– Yes, says Willard, pulling it out from his bindle and handing it over. The Captain inspects it and, seeing the Warden's signature, seems satisfied.

– Have you read it? he says, giving the book back. Either of you?

– Yes, says Willard. We both did. But I – we – we found it … hard to understand.

– Ah, says the Captain. Not uncommon. If you read it again on the crossing, I'll help explain what I can. But you must know where we're going?

Willard senses a final test and wrinkles his brow, stuck for a moment – then it comes to him.

– Nodnol, he says. We're going to Nodnol.

– Very good, says the Captain. Very good.

And with that, he walks down the plank and untethers the rope before re-boarding and sliding the plank up on to the deck. Then he disappears through the door of the bridge and, after a moment's inertia, a rumble starts, a plume of blue smoke and then the boat pulls away from the bank.

III

WELCOME TO THE CORPORATION

YOUR HANDBOOK

Congratulations!

If you are reading this, it means you have most likely reached your ship on time and have received the Handbook from your Captain. If so, you are now about to embark on the next stage of the rest of your life: an exciting new career within the world of the Corporation. Your journey ahead will be filled with many new adventures, but initially it may all seem a little strange. Don't worry if you are a little disoriented at first; this is completely natural.

To help you settle in, and to get the most out of your first few weeks, we recommend that, during the crossing, you study carefully the information contained within this Handbook. Some of what you read may be unfamiliar, but your Captain will do their best to explain any of the more unusual terms. (Please note: if you were already in possession of this Handbook because you are returning to complete your induction, you may be familiar with much of this information. But we request you check with your Captain that your Handbook is up to date, and then re-read it).

In the meantime, sit back and enjoy your sailing. We look forward to welcoming you at Ben-Orkul station when you arrive to go through your contacts.

And remember: work hard, stay positive.

The Corporation team

A BRIEF HISTORY OF MODERN DATA FINANCE

(An introduction by Ali Ben-Orkul)

Welcome!

You will soon be joining the new and exciting world of the Corporation.

When I first joined the Corporation many years ago, it all seemed rather overwhelming – as it must for you now. But what helped me most in the early stages of my own career was an understanding of the unique economic conditions that existed within Nodnol, a set of conditions which have allowed the Corporation to become what it is today. And this knowledge I will now outline for you in the hope that your journey too might, one day, prove as successful as my own.

One of the best economic histories of Nodnol is recorded in a book my father kept on the shelf in his room. It was called *An Introduction to Modern Data-Finance* by Karl Ohm and I used to read that book, enthralled by Ohm's analysis of how data-firms were fast becoming the world's central financial players.

This might seem a rather odd interest for a young boy to possess but, by way of explanation, let me tell you about a flower that grew in our back garden. It was a gentian; bright blue and shaped like a bottle, and it was strange in that it never bloomed. The flower was always closed, its stamen entombed by the bright petals – until one specific insect landed. The insect was the carpenter bee, and could coax the petals open by modulating the buzzing of its wings to a note approximating mid-C. At this, the flower would start to sing, then vibrate and burst open. Pollen would erupt from its anther and the bee could at last climb through, lapping at the nectar inside. It seemed to me that the bee had some spectral tuning fork, a hidden key to open the riches of that flower. And I saw Ohm's book as my hidden key; his insights were to be *my* tuning fork; to unlock the rich but tightly furled world of international data-finance. It was a hollow goal, I'll admit it, but I'd grown up poor and saw no harm in wanting better. I still don't. And neither should you.

Ohm made it clear that some of the richest and most furled worlds of all were to be found among the emerging data-markets of Nodnol's 'third wave of financialisation'. But he also counselled that to be successful when operating in Nodnol's 'third wave', you had to understand how it came about.

His book traced Nodnol's current voraciousness back through three distinct evolutions. The first wave of Nodnol's fiscal awakening began, according to Ohm, in 1855 with the passing of the Limited Liability Act, back when it was still called London. Ohm proposed that this act was essential in laying the foundations for Nodnol's current financial markets as it allowed speculators to do just that – speculate. It meant that shareholders were no longer fully responsible for debts incurred in pursuit of a firm's ventures and, instead, their losses were limited to the value of their shares. Thus, by freeing entrepreneurs from the fear of a debtors' gaol, the huge amounts of capital that had accumulated during the Industrial Revolution were mobilised.

But two world wars put the brakes on this burgeoning new financialisation. In the aftermath of World War II, and with the world economy in ruins, the Americans pegged thirty-five dollars against an ounce of gold at the Bretton-Woods conference to try to stem the hyperinflation running rampant across Europe. It was a brutal financial castration, but it worked as it kept capital locked into markets. Speculators could no longer spark the violent fluctuations and devaluations that had before marred most of the world's major currencies, and it also meant governments could tightly control (and for 'control' here read 'tax') capital flows. And, so tethered, the financial markets stagnated until, in 1963, the second wave began.

The second wave was instigated by a London bank, called Warburg & Co, who were instrumental in the dismantling of the Bretton-Woods Gold Standard. Warburg's secret weapon was a young maverick, a trader called Fraser, who helped the bank to create what was called the Eurobond. In essence, Fraser's Eurobond was a financial instrument that allowed Warburg & Co to lend across international borders while avoiding the tight controls agreed at Bretton-Woods. It was to be drawn on (at least in name) by the Italian state giant Autostrade, and so by manipulating the laxer rules governing bonds held by semi-state companies, Warburg now had an instrument they could sell while circumventing the crippling charges levied under the terms of the Gold Standard. In effect, they had created a new bond that paid interest but was not taxed. It was of course a spectacular success.

And where did Warburg trade these Eurobonds? In London, of course. Like water finding an opening, wealth kept hidden since the War now flowed into London's financial markets once more and, when the traders had taken their cut, then washed back out. The second wave had begun.

This new evolution continued, almost unabated, until things were again curtailed: this time by the crash of 2008. The markets collapsed spectacularly and, when they re-emerged, were bound and tethered by regulation once more. And things may have continued this way – but for the vote on independence.

After the vote, a rechristened and unshackled Nodnol was keen to rediscover the entrepreneurial spirit of Fraser and so it extended an invite to the Corporation; identifying them (and quite rightly) as an essential and visionary mechanism to help jumpstart Nodnol's new spirit of daring entrepreneurialism. The Corporation accepted and the third financial wave began.

The rest, as they say, is history. There is a little more to this story, of course, events that you may come to learn in due time, but for now know this: the best way to become a productive member of the Corporation team is for you too to embrace Fraser's (and Nodnol's) brave new spirit of entrepreneurial derring-do.

Study well what I have outlined here – for it is only through staring back that you may learn to see forward.

And remember: work hard, stay positive.

Ali Ben-Orku

IV

THE RIVER

The Captain is down in the engine room when Nodnol first comes into view.

Willard and Nyla are standing on the front deck, leaning with folded arms on the metal railing, and the ship is sailing down another wide estuary. For hours they have stood in silence, having long given up their hushed and excited questions to instead let ever-wilder images of what might await them spool across their mind's horizon. But neither is prepared for what they now see.

The ship rounds a sharp meander and the city emerges before them. Impenetrable walls of glass now tower along either side of the river, the soaring frontages of countless buildings rising from both banks and packed so tight against each other that you could scarce slip a fist between one building and the next. Willard and Nyla's eyes widen as though they've been dragged into a darkened room.

What is before them now is so distant from everything they have ever known, have ever even thought to know, that their language no longer holds any dominion. They can't articulate the jetties at the base of the towers, structures made of balustrades and tensioned wires supporting cantilevered walkways; or how, up and down the river, the sun is catching on the levees of glass and turning the river a deep orange as the dappling light glitters back from the immeasurable angles of glass. Which of their words could describe how the ghostly outlines of the immense buildings – squared-off pyramids or towers stepped with merlons and crenels or structures widening from base to top like sprouting bromeliads – twinkle like white quartz while everything else, the water and the jetties and the shapes sitting on the horizon behind, are cast with a sepia glow? If the world ever spoke over them before, here it is bellowing. The minutes slip past, fantastic and insistent, but without finding their mark on them the way the normal passing of a moment should, without a ruffle or clip or snag. This is a land beyond their comprehension, and they travel it in silence. But the silence is not tranquil; it is bright and constant, a light when trying to sleep, the inactivity of some incubate power pouring over its own opaque malevolence. And under such a stillness things come up and peck at them, things from their insides that were kept at bay in the Line by the noise and distraction of the running of an ordered world. The city sits upon them, resolute and sullen, riveted to their vision with an atavistic certainty in itself as, against it all, the salty smell of the water drifts past on the breeze. Here it is, every suspicion of more now transposed to fact – but where is this place? What have they blundered into? From what sack escaped some wild wind capable of fashioning all this? The weight of their ignorance compresses their heads.

They glide along dog's teeth of jetties, every so often sailing by the crumbling stumps of masonry where a structure has been ripped down to allow greater access to the waterside, and always the deserted river runs on before them, disappearing around the next snaking bend. And under the watch of the thousands of windows, reflecting the sun in ever-changing colours like giant compound eyes, they scuttle on, pushing on deeper into Nodnol's glittering bowels.

THE GATES

That evening the ship comes to a set of huge solid metal gates which, on some hidden signal from the Captain, slide open with a mechanical whir to admit them. Once they are through, the gates close, locking them in a metal pen.

There is no exit that Willard or Nyla can see, save another set of huge gates high above, and they are wondering how they will reach them when the water begins to pour down from the sides. Willard and Nyla look on open-mouthed, terrified the rising water will submerge and drown them – but they see that the ship rises with the water and their fear subsides. There are three levels to climb and as they wait the Captain comes onto the deck and addresses them, projecting his voice over the pummelling of the water spilling down the metal walls.

– Be vigilant on the next part of our journey, he says. There's been some recent trouble on this stretch; it's not good to sail it in the dark. We'll pass the night in the lock and set off in the morning.

He sees Willard's surprise and adds, in a conspiratorial whisper as if the gushing water might overhear:

– They say they've been left undisturbed too long up there, that they've gone native.

Nyla tries to press him further. At first all he will say is it is treacherous, but then something flickers inside him. He relents a little, shakes his head.

– You must think me awful, he says. The clipboard, the uniform, for not saying more. I know what it must be like for you when you first come from the Line, how confusing it must be. But my contract forbids it. They prefer to do the explaining at the office, when you arrive. But, if I can give you one piece of advice, then it's this: work hard, stay positive. It can all work out well in the end.

And with that the Captain glazes over once more, returning to the engine room and leaving them staring at the cascading water of the lock.

– Offices, Willard says, ships and engines. Cities, corporations, contracts: I can say all these things now, make the noises, but they come out of me empty. The words aren't mine – this whole place is impenetrable.

– We can learn new words, says Nyla.

– Only if we become new people.

– Then that's what we'll do. But let's keep our old ones, hide them somewhere, our bindles and scroggins and tarps. I like them too.

Willard reaches out and takes Nyla by the hand. He wishes he better could describe to her the sound all this is making within him, the coiling spring of each passing moment as it prepares to move out and against the world.

He squeezes.

And when Nyla squeezes back, just as hard, he knows she can hear it too.

THE MOLES

Willard and Nyla sleep on deck that first evening, under a thick blanket, and the river is as dark and still as a sheet of blackened tarp. Not a noise can be heard and more than once Willard wakes to a night so total, so silent, that he lies frozen, immobile on his back and with the slow-horror that he has lost all his senses – until a rippling of water against the hull reassures him he does indeed own his faculties. So placated, he sinks back down into a dreamless oubliette.

He wakes with the dawn the next morning and sees Nyla is already up and dressed, standing at the railing with her gaze fixed on the walls of the lock. The Captain comes on deck, checks they are up, and soon the ship starts moving. But if what they sailed on before was un-riverlike, then what comes next is not a river at all.

Gone are the brighter waters of earlier. Instead, the water here is thicker, murkier and almost viscous, shining with rainbow slicks of something immiscible floating on the surface. And if the buildings earlier had been threatening to break free and overrun themselves, then here they have. Willard stares at the towers above them, higher than ever, lost in banks of low-hanging cloud. Downriver, he thought he could scarce get a fist between each building – here it is a hair. Each structure knitted to the next with scarce a join, like flaps of skin fusing after a laceration.

There are still windows – Willard estimates them in the millions now – but they are no longer square and sitting in rows. Now they creep erratic across the entirety of the immense walls either side of them, clustering here in hexagonal portholes like honeycombs, or running off elsewhere in triangles; the walls above taking on the dendritic patterning of a clustering root system. On both sides of the river, the glass pulses with iridescence, seeming to heave and shrink and breathe. They drift up through the soporific waters under the soaring turrets of glass, hundreds of them, thousands, getting taller and taller and more elaborate, their immense roots buried somewhere deep below the water's edge and their tops scraping at the trout-coloured clouds.

And it is clear they are no longer alone.

At irregular intervals, an unseen door opens and a pale-faced man or woman shuffles out. They all wear smart clothes but look dishevelled: mad-haired, wearing shiny shoes but with broken heels or staggering jacketless, shirts untucked or half-opened with scraps of cloth loosed around their necks in loops. Their eyes are saucerlike and they rub them with knuckles as if the light, weak as it is, is an irritant. Shambling, they creep down to the waterside and drink with cupped hands from the oily coagulant that is floating on the river's surface. Even in drinking, they are never still, pacing and twitching like someone trapped in a room and awaiting important news. When they see the ship, they point and gibber from the water's edge, but Willard and Nyla are too far away to understand any of it, if understand they even could. But unearthly as they are, after such earlier solitude, Willard finds the sight of these degenerates almost nourishing.

– What on earth? Willard says to the Captain, who has come back on deck.

– Moles, he replies. Most are natives, from Nodnol, but some were promoted from the Line, like you, when the Corporation couldn't fill its positions. They are all on training contracts. Accommodation is so expensive they live in the lower vaults of the buildings while they're hoping to be made permanent – but there's only a handful of posts offered each year. The competition is intense; some don't handle it so well.

– Are they dangerous? says Willard.

The Captain looks uncertain.

– No, he says, not as long as we don't get too close. But some of them have lost all grip on what's real. They get frenzied sometimes, particularly if they haven't been able to have a drink in a while. They seem calm for now; we'll keep our eyes open.

– Why are they drinking? Nyla asks, pointing to another mole lapping at the water's edge.

– They get addicted to something in the water, says the Captain. It keeps them going, so they can work for longer without stopping, trying to secure a permanent position. Most don't, of course, but some manage.

Willard tries to press him further, but he shakes his head.

– I'm sorry, he says. I've already said too much.

THE NOTE

The ship slips on; the current quickens.

The sun is high overhead when they round another snaking bend. Willard, watching from the front deck, sees the river widen and soon spots an island splitting the course of the water into two channels. As they approach he studies the island more closely and realises he has at last found something he recognises: it is made of several floating rations containers, held in place by a wire mesh. There is a striped pole fixed on top of the centre-most container. The pole is bent and misshapen and mounted with a pulsing yellow beacon that flickers and flits as they approach. By the base of the pole is a red fuel drum with a wooden board placed on top and, scrawled on the board in hasty lettering, is a faded message:

WELCOME. FUEL FOR YOU. HURRY BUT
BE CAREFUL – MOLES ARE RESTLESS.

They draw up alongside the island and the Captain slows the boat, tethering the hull to a mooring ring set into one of the large stone blocks. He jumps out, telling Willard and Nyla to stay on board, and makes for the fuel. Once he has collected it he disappears below deck, leaving Willard and Nyla to study the sign.

– That's useless, says Nyla. Worse than no sign at all.

Willard agrees.

– Were we not already hurrying? he says. But it doesn't sound good.

There's a low and juddering growl as the engine starts, a rush of bilge water and a bellow of smoke, and then the ship pulls away, leaving the sign to the loneliness of the rocks.

Once they clear the island the current picks up. The sun starts to drop, lighting the lengths of the canyons of glass so the whole gorge glows blue and green and purple like the crystal lacquers of a dragonfly's wings. The landscape becomes spectacular in its uniformity and it's soon impossible for either Willard or Nyla to estimate their progress. They take to picking a single window, somewhere high up, and keeping their eyes fixed on it to gauge their speed. Each pane of glass seems locked into place under sinewy girders and the carapaces either side of the water now look like they are made of skin stretched taut over heaving muscle. The buildings seem alive here, as if they are inhaling and exhaling as ghosts of iridescence ripple along their walls.

On they press.

The sun drops lower, fixed on a track, and the water flames. The sky cross-hatches, spigots of night push down.

NIGHT

The stretch they are on is narrow, winding north. The buildings either side steeple above so, when sun dips below the lip of the western ridge of towers, the darkness lands on them like rain; there are none of the vacillations of dusk they were used to in the Line. The Captain stops the boat and comes up on deck.

– Are we close? asks Nyla.

– Four hours, says the Captain. Maybe six.

– Can't we push on? asks Willard, thinking of the dwindling rations in their packs.

The Captain shakes his head, reminding them of the note, and so it is that Willard and Nyla spend their second night on the river.

The silence is as deep as it was before but this time the darkness is not so absolute. Willard and Nyla lie, holding each other under their blankets, and watch as, high above, lights from the endless banks of windows wink on and off, off and on and on and off, dancing along both sides of the gorge like spectral children chasing each other through the tents of night. They watch the lights and think of the Line – its pinpricks of campfires, its sepulchral deserts with their brutal dome of stars – and how once they called It home.

– Will we really bring our child up here? Willard says, nuzzling himself into the back of Nyla's neck.

– We will, says Nyla. Somehow, we will.

She takes his hand and places it on her stomach. She holds it there so he can feel, as she does, the life inside.

– Would you go back? she says.

– It's too late for that, says Willard.

– But if Mr Hummel appeared, right here now, and said he would take us, would you? Would you go back?

– I don't know, says Willard, pulling her close. How can I know anything anymore?

– I wouldn't, says Nyla. Not even if the Warden herself came on board and begged us. Your mother always said you were stupid for thinking there might be more, something else. But she was wrong. There's more alright; a whole world more, and maybe it's a better world or maybe it's worse – but at least it's the world, and if you can look at me … look at me and swear you could go back, then – then I'll go to the bridge, right now, and I'll make the Captain turn around.

– No, says Willard. We're here now. No going back.

He kisses her head and they fall asleep, tangled together under the cavorting of the lights.

THE FOG

In the morning, they wake to a milk-thick fog.

Willard can see nothing, not even the outline of the huge buildings, can barely make out Nyla beside him, and it is clear that trying to sail in such a whiteout is impossible. They hear the Captain emerge and then shout to them from somewhere down deck.

– Don't worry, he says. It'll lift once the sun rises a bit higher.

– We'll be OK, Willard says to Nyla's outline. We'll still get there today.

But the optimism is short-lived. The narrowness of the river combined with the height of the buildings traps the fog in the gulley and they remain stationary, trapped under the whiteness. Eventually the air thins enough that the smoking censer of the sun becomes briefly visible, darkly globed above, but the fog soon descends again, coming down more thickly than before.

And with this second thickening comes a terrible and rattling wail.

It rises up from the water and then bounds back and forth between the towering walls of the buildings. At first it is low and baleful, a tenebrous dirge, but it rises steadily in pitch, becoming more clamorous and feral until it shoots them both through rigid with fear. Willard finds Nyla and they clamp together, grasping each other as the abysmal screams bound and re-bound between the glass walls of the canyon.

A hand grabs Willard by the shoulder and he turns to see, through the fog, the Captain's face. It is small, shrunken with panic.

– The moles, the Captain says, his voice shaking. We've stopped too long. We must go, it's too narrow here if they decide to wade from the jetties. The fog be damned.

The Captain runs up the deck and they hear a metallic coughing as the engine starts to splutter. The ship gives a series of shuddering lurches before it at last catches with a triumphant roar followed by the acrid smell of smoke, and they start up the river, not able to see the front of the boat from the back. The terrible surfs of screaming rise and break around them and now it's Nyla's turn to grab Willard.

– How will he keep us to the middle? she shouts over the cacophony of screaming.

Willard says nothing, can offer no reassurance because he doubts the Captain too – but for three hours, they creep unhindered through the white veil as abominable howls traverse the mist.

Around midday the shroud lifts, rising up as quickly as it came down, and within fifteen minutes the river is clear. The fog dies off and with it the terrible cries of the moles recede until the river is flat and grey and silent once more.

Willard and Nyla see they are still in a narrow gorge, but now the buildings have changed. Their uppermost towers now lip over the ship in marvellous canopies of overhangs, spectacular cornicing of glass and steel seemingly suspended by nothing but their own inertia and defying all logic. They hear the Captain come back on deck but their gazes are sutured to the overhanging buildings framing the narrow strip of the sky.

THE ATTACK

Willard is still staring upwards when Nyla's scream snaps him from his reverie.

There is a horrendous crash, then another and another, and he turns to see the Captain on his knees near the bridge door, buckled in a paroxysm of pain. He is clutching at his shoulder and Nyla, already beside him, is trying to help him to his feet. But the Captain looks at her and forces two sentences out through the shaking of his groans.

– Take the wheel. Leave me and take the wheel, damn it, or we're all dead.

Another series of dreadful thumps and crashes erupt. There is a heavy pummelling on the ship and Willard turns, watching in dismay as something rips a jagged hole in the deck before exploding in shrapnel of wheels and levers.

– The moles, the Captain shouts, hoping Nyla can still hear him. They're throwing things down from the buildings, take the bloody wheel.

Nyla looks at him in horror, is fixed to the spot and unable to move.

– The bridge, he says. Inside it is the wheel and beside that a lever, the throttle. Find it, push it all the way forward and then keep us in the middle of the channel. You can do it, he says. You must.

Nyla gathers herself, stands and makes a run for the bridge – but is knocked off balance as a huge wooden table lands in the water with a ferocious white depth-charge, rocking the hull over and back. She gets back to her feet, wooden missiles shattering to splinters all around her, and this time makes it inside and grabs the throttle. She rams it up and urges the boat out of the abominable stretch of overhangs, daring not look anywhere but straight ahead to where the river widens.

Willard is thrown backward by the acceleration but manages to stagger across the deck to the Captain. He bends down, catching him under the arms, but the Captain is a dead weight and Willard is forced to widen out his legs as he tries to drag him to safety. Another huge thump batters a dent in the steel awning above the bridge and this time Willard hears something bounce onto the deck. He changes direction, zig-zagging through another violent hail of missiles as he pulls the Captain towards the awning – but the Captain becomes animated, starts to writhe, and Willard is forced to release him.

With a trembling arm, the Captain takes something out from inside his shirt and pushes it into Willard's chest. At first, Willard thinks it just the Handbook, but then he realises it's thicker, much thicker, something altogether more sinister.

– This is what the moles are after, the Captain hisses up to Willard through bloodied lips. Take it and tell them.

– Tell who? says Willard, trying to re-set his grip on the Captain's body. Tell who what?

– Everyone, says the Captain. Anyone. I came to Nodnol because I believed in our mission, that we were bringing edifice, enlightenment … but all we're doing is – *this* –

and here, and with a great effort, the Captain raises an arm and points to the buildings towering all around.

– So read it and tell them, tell them all, bring it crashing down around their ears. Tell them that *this* – *this* is all the love they bear you.

Before Willard can respond he hears a wild scream, starting far away but changing in pitch and growing louder and louder until the ship is struck with a sickening force. He stumbles backwards again, this time tripping over something large and landing on his back. He looks at his feet – and finds himself staring at the lifeless body of a mole, face down on the deck and with its head battered flat.

There is another dreadful cry and a second enormous splash rocks the boat from side to side, but, when Willard pulls himself upright, this time he sees not a table floating in the water but another mole. And it is alive, scrabbling at the ship's hull like a drowning insect as it tries to climb aboard. For a moment he is frozen, held in horror by the dreadful scraping of its ossified fingernails on the ship's metal, but manages to shake himself free.

Willard looks around, grabs up a splintered section of table leg and, cudgel in hand, sprints to the ship's edge where, using every muscle in his upper body, he raises back an arm before smashing the mole right into its hollow alabaster face. The cheekbones offer resistance – then cave in, and the mole releases its frenzied grip on the ship's side with a gurgling shriek, falling back with a splash and floating lifelessly off downriver.

With the mole gone, Willard at last returns for the Captain. He catches him by the legs and, with a huge effort, manages to drag him into the relative safety of the bridge. Nyla is there, focused ahead, unwavering, and Willard crosses the bridge-floor to stand tight beside her, urging her to keep gunning on the throttle. It's ten more minutes before they clear the narrowest excesses of that dreadful tunnel, each one a terrible span of erratic battering on the hull, but slowly the water widens. The pummelling dies away, the river quietens.

And on the horizon they see something grow from the distant wall of buildings: a towering spike standing out proud from even the hugeness of the glass walls around it. It's a blazing menhir, shining like a beacon, and on the jetty in front is tied a long and thin flag waving in furious semaphore. And only then do they start to breathe again because they know they have survived, have reached their final destination. Willard leaves Nyla's side to go reassure the Captain – and that is when he notices he is dead. Stone dead, a trickle of dark blood coming from his ear.

And what does Willard do?

First, he laughs, laughs uncontrollably, laughs and shakes and screams. Then he goes back to the bridge and, with Nyla pushing the throttle ever onwards, opens the book and begins to read aloud.

V

THE LINE

FROM ORIGIN TO APPLICATION. A TREATISE
FOR A NEW WORLD ORDER.

Lila Bonkuer

Abstract

This paper sets out how we might use 'big data' to offer
a solution for the current volatility which is having a pro-
nounced and negative impact on international markets.

It identifies a need to eradicate this volatility because
a) it is eradicable and b) it significantly reduces world
growth capabilities (in particular, the GDP potential of the
more developed Afro-Hispanic economies).

This paper finds that current Afro-Hispanic data-
finance operations are, when considered on a global scale,
net beneficial and so should continue. However, it does
identify (though does not apportion blame towards) the
Corporation and other such data-finance institutions as
having helped create current volatility.

This paper describes how the current model of data-
finance has inadvertently increased current geo-political

uncertainty by facilitating 1) the economic collapses of Nodnol, and then 2) the subsequent economic collapse of other major cities. It attributes these collapses to the widespread take-up of Nodnol's post-independence economic policy – what is often called the *'third wave of financialisation'* (Ohm, K.). It contests that this policy, while initially successful, ultimately led to an unforeseen 'hollowing out'[1] of many major urban centres in both Europe and North America.

However, this paper does not see the current situation as being a *direct result* of data-finance operations. While it acknowledges the role of such operations in creating the current geo-political situation, this paper contests that migrants have been made homeless, or at least extremely precariously tenured, due to domestic governments over-extending land to foreign investors and, as such, are being forced into crossing borders they would otherwise not choose to cross by *political* and *not economic* policy.

Therefore, due to the overwhelming net global benefits that the 'third wave' financial model has created for the world economy, this paper does not see the solution as a curtailment of Afro-Hispanic operations within Europe and America.

Instead, it proposes a more elegant and market-based solution.

---

1. *Hollowing out* here is defined as 'an artificially accelerated process where the majority of residents in an urban centre leave in search of affordable accommodation, thus turning large sections of residential land over to data-firms for operational development'.

Part 1: A Rationale for Change

1.1 The Scale of Our Current Problem
Africa 'Creaking at the Seams' according to Kwoabo[2]

'If Africa cannot act together and as one to persuade a sig-nificant majority of its citizens that it can gain control of its migratory crisis, then the African State of Nations will find itself at the mercy of a populist uprising, which is already stirring,' said Jean-Baptiste Kwoabo, head of the Congolese Secret Services.

Noting that the number of migrants entering Africa in the wake of Nodnol's vote for independence could soon run into the millions, Kwoabo added that this was 'the first roll of the dice in a bigger geopolitical game. We'll soon sink under the weight of an ever-increasing infestation of Nodnollers fleeing from economic devastation.' The only solution to the crisis, said Kwoabo, 'is to remove the gravi-tational pull' causing the waves of European and American migrants to enter African and Latin regions in the first place.

2. Africa 'Creaking at the Seams' – *first posted on Info-Assassin.*

Earlier this month, a Syrian army chief warned that the risk of social unrest in the Middle East would intensify if something was not done to stem the flows of immigrants from Frankfurt and Paris in the wake of the the spectacular collapse of the cities' economies after what he called 'flagrant overexposure to a short-sighted and chronically ill model which relied on rapacious foreign investment'. He added, 'We assumed European cities were rational actors with an eye on their own long-term interests. Unfortunately, this assumption was wrong' and he urged Syrian citizens to now consider arming themselves.

Top Mexican security experts warned President Gerardo Chilla last October that the Hispanic middle class across the regions was becoming 'radicalised' as a result of his open-borders migrant policy, and that domestic disorder could ensue as a result. They demanded the Wall be built imme-diately, adding, 'You get what you vote for. The Americans have no one to blame but themselves.'

The world is in crisis. And it is a crisis against which the state (or, rather *states* in their many manifestations) is fight-ing rather ineptly.

The crisis is, of course, migration. 'Swarms' of migrants are being displaced from the cities of Europe and North America and pouring into Africa and South America as the economically disenfranchised are drawn inexorably towards the prosperity of more developed nations.

Immigration is now THE key issue for all Tropical-region political parties and it is ripping previously stable governments apart. Where once the parameters of immigration controls were dictated by government policy, now the parameters of government policy are dictated by immigration; resettlement quotas being foisted on the Congo, boats patrolling the Mexican Gulf, burning historic landing cards, fences, a wall across the Rio Grande.

And none of it is working. None of it can work. The pull is simply too strong. The bigger the walls that are built, the higher people are prepared to jump.

But there is a solution. For although the state may wish to ruin us, it is the market that can lead us to freedom.

1.2 The Rise of the Corporation

To understand how we might solve our current issues, we must first understand how we arrived here. Therefore, an honest appraisal of the role of the Corporation in the spreading of the 'third wave' is essential to having a meaningful grasp of the current geo-political problem.

After the vote for Independence, Nodnol found it increasingly difficult to attract investment. The Americans, having their own problems with Beijing, had curtailed international spending and Europe, given the outcome of the vote, was hostile. In short, the Nodnol economy was flatlining.

In response, the Chancellor tried to defibrillate by relaxing regulations governing non-domestic currency transactions, and Nodnol set about attracting whatever investment they could get. And it worked. There followed a period of rapid economic growth as new apartment blocks were signed off all over the city, high-end structures of wall-to-wall glass to catch the eye of the new investors, and soon foreign capital was buying up accommodation from Kilburn to Kensington (money which the Nodnol exchequer were only too happy to sanction, and which Nodnol banks were only too happy to process).

But so much unplanned glass had an unforeseen consequence. In the summer, the sun reflected back and forth at odd angles between the buildings, and on each reflection the rays became stronger and more concentrated, as if being focused by a magnifying glass. Things began melting: roads running to tar, trees bursting into flame and electric cables fusing, and while this was initially ignored as an annoyance, the first legal proceedings were initiated when a Baroness's penthouse went up in flames. But it was all a legal Gordian knot: insurers invoking Apollo clauses, building contractors blaming architects, architects blaming planning regulations and planning regulators blaming the building contractors. There were claims and counterclaims as plaintiffs performed ever-more gymnastic wranglings to try and prove it was actually refraction causing the issue and not, in fact, reflection.

And so it may all have remained, nothing more than a protracted legal headache, if it wasn't for one of the first data-firms attracted to the newly independent Nodnol, a Congolese venture called the Corporation.

In the beginning, the Corporation was little more than a fly-by-night analytics firm set up in a small office a few miles south of the Thames. But the vision of one of one of its young analysts, a gifted maverick called Ali Ben-Orkul, changed its fortunes. Ben-Orkul saw in the legal mess an opportunity. First, he raised an antiquated statute allowing the firm to bring the whole city to court as a single litigant and, after being awarded a huge settlement, convinced them to invest it in buying data. He bought hordes and hordes of it, from anywhere and everywhere possible: lists from cash-strapped health care trusts and local authorities, social media companies, smart phone apps, dark-web exchanges. Finally, he fed it all into an algorithm he'd built, one that was able to generate sizeable returns by triangulating the optimal ratio of a neighbourhood's chicken shops to sourdough bakeries to predict the most lucrative investment properties. Within a year, the Corporation had moved to the Square Mile and built itself an impressive place fronting the river, employing over a thousand people.

And it was from here that Ben-Orkul was able to give the Corporation a new and single goal, a goal that was both breathtakingly simple and ambitious.

He recognised that harvesting data was no longer a means to a financial end but was now a financial end in itself, an asset in its own right, to rival oil or gold. Ben-Orkul saw that, with enough data, the Corporation could guarantee a return on its investments – every single time. So he re-focused the Corporation to operate on one simple premise: *data must lead to action*. To him, all that was needed for successful speculation was data, seeing the model of using traders for investments as no better than monkeys bashing at buttons. He wanted to bypass the traditional European method of financial trading, practices he saw as intransigent, systems that were benighted and far too reliant on the old investment models. The Corporation didn't need traders, he concluded, it simply needed analysts.

But what *really* differentiated Ben-Orkul's vison for the Corporation from more traditional West Coast companies was that he wasn't looking to make a profit by harvesting data to sell to third parties. Instead, Ben-Orkul understood that the Corporation could make *thousands of times* more by harvesting data to steer *its own* investments.

The modern era of data-finance was born, and it was owned by a Congolese firm who'd cut out the Western middlemen.

1.3 Nodnol: A Case Study in Data-Finance and Displacement

Re-born and re-branded, the Corporation had a seismic impact on Nodnol.

The first thing Ben-Orkul did was to lobby the Department for Environment, Food and Rural Affairs to lower the minimum salinity required for a stretch of water to be classified as the open ocean. And the Minister, assured the Corporation would pay a hefty annual levy, agreed.

Why did Ben-Orkul pursue this lobby? The answer is ingenious: under the new regulation, a section of the Corporation's office situated on the tidal section of the Thames (the section that happened to house its accounts department) was now considered to be operating in international waters – meaning, of course, no tax liability. Within a year, data-firms from all across first Africa and then Latin America had established offices on the river, shining towers studding both sides of the waterway. And around all this Nodnol became a gorging gullet, growing fat on capital.

Seeing the streams of investment pouring in to Nodnol, other major financial centres followed suit, and soon cities around Europe and America were similarly de-regulating to try and attract the proliferation of new data-finance firms. But, just as the 'third wave' was going global, it began to emerge that economic operations in Nodnol were changing not just the fiscal landscape of the city but its physical landscape too.

At first it was just more and more grey motorway, miles and miles of concrete overpasses and slip-roads to fast-track foreign financiers into the city centre. But then, from the flanks of the nondescript suburban scrub grew glittering buildings. They were the headquarters of tech giants, the huge box shapes of outsourced server farms and internet delivery warehouses or the luminous frontages of hotels, all set up to serve the massive influx of data-financiers. The main roads between these buildings became walls of electronic billboards, flickering and dancing as adverts were tailored – smiling women, pristine beaches, men in towels – to match each passing phone signal.

And there followed another, more detrimental, transformation. Between all the new developments, the shells of empty buildings began to appear: boarded-up shops and pubs and abandoned cars sinking into the tarmac of the darkened side streets on empty tyres, never a soul to be seen. This decay was confined, at first, to areas near the river – but gradually neighbourhoods farther back began to undergo the same ghostly metamorphosis as ever more land was bought up by multinationals, each hoping to turn some coin from the explosion of data-firms all along the waterfront. This didn't go unnoticed, but the assumption by policy-makers was that the benefits of these investments would soon trickle down and kick-start a wholesale regeneration.

However, the predicted redistribution of wealth into the wider economy was curtailed by a peculiar architectural quirk – the fact that nearly all new developments in Nodnol had been designed with a network of underpasses connecting straight to airports or train stations.

Above ground, the thousands of ill-conceived towers of glass were causing more trouble than ever. Increasing swathes of the city were now being scorched, so spending even short amounts of time on the streets became dangerous. And Ben-Orkul's legal victory had set a precedent. Now, anyone lucky enough not to see their own property melt was just as likely to be summoned as a witness in some third-party claim. The risk of becoming embroiled in such a prolonged legal dispute was simply too great, and people just stayed in the tunnels.

It was true that money was pouring into Nodnol like never before, that throngs of data-firm employees flew in and out for work, and bought up properties across the city. But while they were in Nodnol they all moved around through the underpasses. The influx of new data-financiers spent fortunes in cafés, gyms, and supermarkets, but they did it without ever setting foot in the actual communities in which they 'lived'.

Local neighbourhoods disintegrated – but investors kept driving the rent up until anyone who wanted to live in a suburb within five miles of the river couldn't afford it and anyone who *could* afford it didn't want to. There were whole apartment blocks whose most lucrative selling point became the fact that no one had to actually live there because it was so easy to get everywhere else. Entire boroughs became just roundabouts and petrol stations, others a monotony of offices framing stone plazas, each with a manicured garden of date palms and hydrangeas turned a vivid blue from being kept in pots of acidic soil. The pristine lobbies all hung with the aromas of newly completed building work, of fresh concrete or painted shuttering and disinfectant, all the smells signalling an economy seemingly keeping its lower orders engaged.

But in between all the sparkling foyers and the sprinkler-fed lawns, more and more empty streets emerged as Nodnollians poured abroad to try find affordable accommodation, road after road becoming just another withered capillary of asphalt around the base of one of Nodnol's pulsing financial veins. Whole swathes cleared out, leaving the pitiable spectacle of Nodnol's spectral neighbourhoods hidden behind its shining frontages.

The third wave had indeed allowed Nodnol to become fully independent, to be financially autonomous and to act as it wished. But it turned out such independence came at a cost: Nodnol could only pay for all this sovereignty by selling every square inch of itself. Financial policy had long ago given us the shell company – now it had given us the first shell city.[3]

---

3. But not the last. It is perhaps worth noting here what Grogan and Lowry identify as the defining indicators of a shell city:

> *Cities were first established as a means by which inhabitants, by banding together geographically, could pool a range of resources and therefore benefit from the associated economies of scale. Early cities were socio-democratic by their very nature: they were fiscal entities which were established, and then grown and cultivated, to serve their inhabitants. However, during the third wave, the whole concept of the city changed. A city was no longer seen as a socio-economic entity designed for the benefit of individual inhabitants, rather the opposite view emerged. Inhabitants were now seen as bio-economic units who should work for the benefit of the larger whole. Where first cities were grown to feed their citizens, now it was the other way around.*

Lowry goes further. He describes this tendency of any large economic or financial institution to eventually supersede the individuals from which it is compromised as 'transcendence'. He concludes that

> *just like large cities, large economies also undergo a transcendence once they reach a critical velocity. That is, at some point an economy become so complex and ill-understood that it transcends the very people who participate in it, it instead begins to exist in and of itself. It seems that Friedrich Hayek may have been correct: it is indeed the curious task of modern economics to demonstrate to us how little we truly know of what we imagine we can design.*

VI

THE MANAGER

Willard stops reading and looks up to see the ship is now bearing down on the jetty.

There is a man standing under the flag and calling them in to land, waving both hands high over his head and they can tell even from a little way off that he is different from the Captain. He sports a beard that is neat and impossibly well shaped. His trousers and jacket are made of some luxurious material, with sharp creases along the legs. He wears a heavy gold ornament on his wrist, over his sleeve, a declaration that he is committed to the collection of such things the way some in the Line use to collect unusual stones and hang them from strings on their tents.

– Here. Here. Throw in the rope, he calls as the ship approaches and Willard obliges, heaving the heavy coil of the mooring line overarm so it spins through the air and then slaps down onto the jetty.

Nyla cuts the throttle as the man ties the rope fast to a concrete bollard set like a mushroom and then hops on board.

– I'm so glad you made it, he says, opening his arms as if to welcome Willard in an embrace.

Willard doesn't know what to make of him. He is certainly gaudy and irrepressible, one more riddle for them to solve at the farthest reaches of this farthest river, but he is also animated by a fantastic energy, a terrifying conviction he seems to carry in the certainty of all his certainties. Willard looks on, incredulous, and then at Nyla whose raised eyebrow confirms that she too suspects the same: the man – the Manager of this station, he tells them – is a knave, a simpering idiot who is babbling platitudes in their ears like a brook.

– Never mind all that, Nyla says, we were attacked. Nearly fucking killed.

– Ah, the Manager says, his face lit by a mooning smile. He turns to survey the ship and sees the Captain. Ah, he says again. The moles. A shame. A shame. They're harmless really.

– Harmless, says Willard, poking a foot at the lifeless body of the Captain.

– They are, you know. But they don't like new arrivals. They think of you as competition. The Manager stops. His eyes narrow and he fixes Willard with an odd look.

– You didn't find something, did you? Something you weren't meant to?

– No, says Willard, looking to Nyla.

– What? she says.

– Never mind, says the Manager. Never mind.

The Manager bends over and grabs the Captain by the ankles, dragging him to the edge of the boat. He frisks his pockets, checking inside his shirt, then rolls him with a grunt and pitches his lifeless body into the water. It hits the surface with a slap and bobs there ignobly.

– Death should not be welcomed but never feared. *Let be be finale of seem*, he mutters as his hands cut the air in the shapes of ampersands.

The Manager leads Willard and Nyla off the ship, down the pier and through a revolving door set in the foot of the monolith of glass. They enter a colossal atrium with huge pillars supporting struts spanning the massive dome of the roof. As they walk, Willard rubs his hand over a pillar, feels it is not made of hard metal or secured with bolts and rivets, but instead, like the earlier frontages, seems comprised of a seamless span of a taut, webbed material like the skin between his own fingers. The whole atrium pulses with colour, a pale light that comes directly from the fleshy walls all around.

– Welcome to the Corporation, says the Manager, waving out an arm. Ben-Orkul built all this. Grew it.

– Ben-Orkul? says Willard.

–*Ali* Ben-Orkul? You *have* read the Handbook?

Willard nods and the Manager lets out an unapologetic guffaw.

– Good. Well, when Ben-Orkul came up here first, he could see how big things were going to get. He understood that the Corporation was going to need to grow, and grow fast. And he realised that was the key – growth.

– The Corporation? says Nyla.

– Yes, says the Manager, wringing his hands. Not the brand: growing the actual buildings themselves. He created two new synthetic DNA bases and thus expanded the functional genetic alphabet from four letters to six. The different shape of the new helix he created –

He sees the vacancy taking hold on both their faces and stops.

– Of course, of course. You've only arrived. I suppose this must all sound rather strange. Look, all you really need to know is Ben-Orkul used his modifications to grow a synthetic tissue which allowed organic cells to fuse with silicon-based materials, namely glass. And the results – he waves another arm – well, you've seen the results. So, when I say he grew all this I mean he *grew it*. The buildings here are alive. Truly alive. They grow and plan and run themselves. That oil you saw on the water is an enzyme the tissues secrete as they grow, and the moles, well, they rather like it.

– But your note said they are restless, says Willard.

The Manager looks a bit sunken that Willard has poked a hole in the paper kite he had been flying.

– Yes, about that. The moles – no, sorry, *harvesters* – work for us gathering data, which is sent to the analysts on the top floors. The analysts pump it all into one of Ben-Orkul's algorithms and the algorithm tells us what trades to make. We hit enter, in flows the profit. And it's the profits that fuel the buildings. The more profit, the more the buildings can grow – and the more enzyme they release in the process. And so the harvesters hunt ever harder for data in order to release ever more of the enzyme. It's all quite marvellous. But the current intake of harvesters isn't performing so well. They're tired, coming to the end of their internships, and we only have a few permanent positions. And that's where you come in! We need some good new interns and soon, so we're starting our recruitment.

– You want us to be …Willard pauses, uncertain … to be the things we saw on the river?

– God, no, says the manger. Those are a minority. A tiny minority. It's unfortunate you had to see them at all: they grossly misrepresent us.

– What happens to the others? says Nyla. The harvesters who don't make it?

– I'm glad you asked, says the Manager. I like to show all our new recruits – it does wonders for their motivation.

He stops and points overhead. Looking up, Willard and Nyla see hundreds of wizened bodies hanging on ropes from the highest parts of the atrium. They are naked, dangling from the ankles so their hands fall like willow branches, their skin an ivory white. They are wrinkled like fruit left too long in the basket but despite their disfigurements they are still easily identifiable as moles. When the light pulses through the inner skin of the atrium they shake and sway, paper streamers announcing them to the house of the damned. The Manager jerks a finger towards a dark corner of the ceiling. Willard and Nyla turn their head to follow his pointing but fail to see whatever he is trying to draw their attention towards, give him a blank look.

– Higher, he says, right up in the corner.

This time they see it.

At first it is difficult for them to make out the shapes in the shadows but, the longer they stare, the clearer it becomes until there can be no doubt. There are at least a half-dozen moles in the corner, even more wizened and disfigured than the rest. They have been absorbed into the walls up to their waists, some to their oxters so just their torsos and heads protrude. Their skin has lost the bright-whiteness of the others, is a mackerelled grey, and their faces are contorted and warped, but from such a distance it is hard to tell the exact nature of the contortions.

– Those who don't get offered a permanent position with us have usually incurred significant costs from the lodgings we give them, costs that must be repaid. We find that the fairest way for all parties to proceed is if we … *absorb* their debts.

– It's eating them! gasps Nyla.

– Let's not get into semantics, says the Manager, flicking a wrist. Here in Nodnol we're committed to affording all our trainees the opportunity to become productive members of the economy.

Willard and Nyla say nothing, still staring up at the cocooned pods of the moles being sucked into the very walls of the building. The Manager starts walking again and, after letting him open up a gap, they have to jog to catch up. Soon they reach the end of the atrium and step through a silver arch into a monumental open-air square.

– Well, he says, here I must leave you. I have work to do. Always work to do. Keep going until you reach the cable-car – it'll take you up to Inductions, they'll go through all the paperwork with you.

Willard and Nyla look at the Manager to see if he is joking but he takes a theatrical bow, scraping his hand on the floor, and then scampers away. He stops a little way across the atrium before turning and shouting:

– Remember, work hard. Stay positive and work hard.

But Willard and Nyla are not listening. They have already walked outside to escape the gibberish coagulating in their ears.

THE CABLE-CAR

The square is long and narrow, a grey-paved rectangle flanked by glass fronts, and Willard and Nyla pass through it, crossing over two metal tracks set close together, the type Willard remembers crossing in a town they passed through long ago.

They enter a large grassy expanse and turn left, following the only path, a diagonal line of sandstone slabs, past a line of benches interspersed with purpling flower beds before reaching a small lake. Stopping by the lake, Nyla pulls her shirt-sleeve down over the heel of her hand to wipe the wooden slats of a bench before she sits down and Willard does the same.

There is a large poster draped on the wall behind the lake, top to ground, and they both stare at it for a long time. It depicts a huge, orange bonfire in the middle of a darkening mountain. Around the fire dance people in

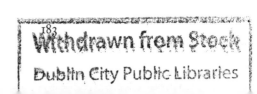
183

odd costumes, girls in red pinafore dresses with billowing white sleeves being twirled through the dark by black-hatted boys. Across the mountains are other bonfires, little orange blobs set high in the purple shadows and mirrored in the lighter purple of the still surface of the lakes below. At the centre of the picture are two silhouetted figures, both staring into the huge fire. At first the scene seems to them an idyll of a time long gone, but the longer they stare, the more they can feel there is something else there, something darker. They keep staring until the colours, the dull olives and deep plums and magentas, merge and swim before them as if they have screwed their eyes tight shut. Looking at the picture is like running their fingers across words etched in a stone; they feel there is a message there but they're unable to get at the sense of it. After a long time, they give up and follow the path out of the garden and there find a sign saying *cable-car*.

It is waiting at the base of the wall, which is not perpendicular, but runs up and away from them at a steep angle. Willard looks up the steep slope as far as he can, but the top floors are so far above they are lost to him in a mixture of glinting and haze from the heat as it rises off the glass.

The cable-car is made of two passenger carriages attached by a steel line and both carriages running up along the wall of the building on a single track. Although Willard can't see the second car, it is clear the system is designed so that each carriage acts as a counterweight to the other: one descends so the other will be hoisted up the steep face; one ascends so it will slow the other coming down. Halfway up the face Willard can see the telltale solitary double-tracked passing point that allows both carriages to slide past each other when otherwise they would be certain to crash. Two carriages tethered together, traversing the same single span, and yet never they are to meet. Willard looks up the track as far as he can and then back to Nyla.

– No going back, he says.

Nyla gives him a weak smile.

– No, no going back.

They get in and up they go, leaving the garden and the square far behind.

Up and up they go, up and up. At first, looking down is dizzying, but soon they climb so high that the whole tributary comes into view, a snaking line of silver curling through the gorge they had just sailed, and as they go even higher, they can follow where the tributary joins the main waterway, clearly delineated due to the reduced size and density of the waterfront buildings. Then they can see the whole river and then the whole city – the two halves of black and grey suburban desert held together by the silver zip of the river running across its midriff. Still up they go and then their vertigo fades, the ground dropping so far away it becomes no more than a painting, so remote that the prospect of falling becomes but a story of a fall they have heard once rather than a real danger in itself. Still up they go, and up even more, until the car eases to a stop and the door flips open on a hinge.

Nyla steps out first and Willard after her, walking onto a wooden terrace. It has rained earlier and water is beaded on the terrace, in thousands of tiny puddles along the lengths of wood. Willard follows Nyla, watching as she disturbs the puddles as she passes, and he lets her lead him through two rows of plants until they emerge onto an open seating area populated by wooden seats and a wrought-iron table. In front of them is a set of double doors and then a corridor, long and windowless, with a single doorway at the end.

They move down the corridor, the carpet cushioning their footsteps. The walls pulse, even more vividly than they had below and, when Nyla reaches the door, she pauses to look at Willard, not so much searching for affirmation but more to afford the moment the gravitas it must surely demand.

He gestures feebly. Nyla grabs the handle and pushes it open.

THE ADMINISTRATOR

In front of them is a woman.

She is a wraith, a mist. Had they not been looking for her, they might have mistaken her for a broom handle.

She is standing in the middle of a nest of papers, loose sheets strewn all over the desk beside her and spread haphazardly across the floor. They have caught her searching for something, and she looks up, angry, crazed, as if being in Nodnol so long has devolved her somehow, driven her wild. Sweat covers the pate of her skull, visible through her thinning hair, and her eyebrows are thin. She wears a pair of horn-rimmed glasses. Willard thinks she means to shout at them – but then the light goes out of her.

– I'm the Administrator, she says, And you're late. Very late.

She clears a space on the desk and sits down on a chair behind, indicating Nyla and Willard should do the same by pointing to the two chairs opposite. Once they are settled, she leans forward and puts her hands on the table, dropping her voice.

– The Corporation is growing so fast we can scarce feed it quick enough. The harvesters are mining data overtime but it's not enough, it's never enough.

She stops speaking. The pulsing light coming from the webbed skin of the office quickens and she turns, looks out her window at the damasked river running far below them like a thread of yarn. She turns back to Willard and Nyla, her eyes fevered again.

– But we've nearly cracked it. We've built the perfect algorithm. The problem is the data. We need more. It's not *pure* enough, it never is, because it records all our biases, all our foibles and failings, all the bots interacting with other bots until what we end up harvesting is the wittering of a less-perfect algorithm running on even worse data that was itself gathered by a more inferior process – on and on like the never-ending branches of a fractal …

Willard coughs into his hand, an attempt to break a twig and scare away whatever fervour is taking hold of her. For a moment it seems too late, that the Administrator is lost in the remote circuitry pulsing through the walls around them – but she sobers, pushes her glasses back up her nose, and continues.

– And that is why you are here. The Corporation needs more harvesters. Better harvesters. We received your letter of recommendation from the Warden. The fact you had read the Handbook already – well, we were impressed, it showed initiative, that we could get up to speed. So we've decided to offer you a promotion, from the Line. Now, if you can read and sign these …

She slides a few stapled sheets of paper across the desk towards them.

– What are they? says Nyla.

– Your contracts.

– Contracts?

The Administrator sighs like a beleaguered parent. This time, when she continues, she speaks slowly.

– For your new posts with us. As entry-level harvesters. Trainees, in the first instance, but it's all outlined in there. So, if you can *please* read and then sign on pages three and five –

– What if we don't want to? says Willard.

– Don't want to what? says the Administrator.

– Sign it, says Willard.

– Well it's up to you, she says, raising her voice and leaning forward in her chair so she is speaking into a small box on her desk. Completely and utterly *your choice* of course. But we can't send you back, not now. You can appreciate it's much too late for all that. So no, you don't *have to* sign it. But if you decide not to take up the harvester position with us today, well, then the other options are – and here she drops her voice and leans towards them – *sub-optimal.*

– Sub-optimal? says Willard.

– Yes, says the Administrator. Sub-optimal.

And she leaves the word to hang in the air. Then she gets up, goes over to a shelf on the wall and starts sorting papers from one pile into another.

– She's mad, Nyla whispers to Willard.

– She's warped alright, Willard whispers back. Being up this river has rotted her. I don't want to be one of those … *things.*

Nyla shudders as she remembers the moles in the wall.

– Neither do I. But if we don't sign then it's … sub-optimal. And I really don't like the sound of sub-optimal.

The woman returns to her seat and looks at them with a smile.

– So have we decided? Are we signing today?

Willard looks at Nyla and she mouths at him slowly, *No. Going. Back.*

– Yes, says Willard, turning back to the Administrator.

The Administrator looks at Nyla.

– Yes, says Nyla. We are signing.

– Excellent, says the Administrator. Perhaps then it's quicker if I read you the terms … ok … so, *you understand that, in signing, you are hereby contracted to the Corporation. You understand that the post is temporary in the first instance but, depending on performance, at the end of your training period may lead to a permanent post. You understand that you are expected to meet all performance targets during said training period and that failure to do so may result in dismissal. You understand that if dismissed or not made permanent then returning to the Line is not permitted. You understand that there will be no remuneration for the duration of said training period, which will last no less than three years and no more than five. You understand that you will be given accommodation in the Corporation, the cost of which will be deducted from your salary should you become permanent, but if you are not made permanent these costs must still be repaid by you and in full. You understand that any and all other costs incurred will also be at your own expense. You understand that you may be required to carry out any and all tasks that the Corporation may deem necessary, regardless of their remit or hours under which they fall. You confirm you have no dependants under five who will be left un-provisioned in your absence. You confirm that, to the best of your knowledge, you have no physical ailment or disability, including, but by no means limited to, scabies, rabies, scurvy or rickets. You confirm you are not pregnant. You confirm that you —*

— But I am pregnant! blurts Nyla.

The Administrator stops reading, opens and closes her mouth like a fish washed up on a riverbank.

– I'm sorry, she says. No one's done that – for a long time. What did you say?

– I'm pregnant, says Nyla again.

– I see, she says, taking up yet another set of papers and flicking through it. Well, it's not mentioned here. Are you sure?

– Certain. Nearly four months.

– Is this true? she says, looking at Willard.

– Yes, Willard says. Is that bad?

– Could be, says the Administrator. Please, a minute. This is most unusual.

She turns in her chair and pulls out a drawer from a metal cabinet, walking her fingers along the top of the files until, after a few false starts, she selects the one she was looking for and removes it. She turns back to the desk, takes the file out from its plastic covering and begins skimming through it, muttering to herself as she goes. Nyla starts to whisper to Willard, but the Administrator holds up her hand and, with a curt *sshhh*, continues to skim the file.

– Aha, she says at last. Aha, as I thought.

– What? says Nyla. What?

– Look, she says, turning the file around to face Nyla and pointing to a short, bullet-pointed paragraph near the bottom of the page. Here.

Nyla begins to read out loud, her mouth tripping over the words:

Directive 22.B: To counteract current concerns about declining birth-rates in the Line, in the unlikely event it should transpire at interview that a prospective candidate (and/or their spouse or significant other) is pregnant or is leaving un-provisioned dependants under five, they should be encouraged (but not obliged) to return to the Line, where every effort will be made to assist their re-integration by subsequently filling out an 'unexpected declaration' form and returning it to the relevant authority, no later than one (1) week after departure. The candidates may, if they choose, decide to continue with the application, but only on the proviso that they forfeit any dependants (whether current or soon-to-be born) to the care of the Corporation. If they choose to return to the Line, they may keep a copy of the Corporation's Handbook as evidence of their unfinished interview and, once all dependants are of an age of self-sufficiency, candidates may return to finish their interview at a time of their choosing by declaring their Handbook to the nearest Warden and asking to speak to Ali Ben-Orkul. While returned to the Line, they must adhere to a strict non-disclosure policy; the penalty for breaching said policy will be either a) declared an Unplacing and skinned alive or b) being burned inside their tent, as to be determined by the relevant Elder.

Nyla finishes reading and the woman snaps the file shut and then leans back in his chair.

– So, there you have it, she says. Follow me or go back, the choice is yours, yours alone. Work or return to – and at the mention of the next name she shudders – *the Line*, if you can bear it. But if you do go back, then remember: not a word. Absolute silence.

She stops and gives Willard a withering look over her glasses.

– I see from your file we told the same thing to your parents, Mr Trophy, when *their* interview was also curtailed. But your father couldn't help himself, it seems. And we don't want a repeat of all that.

With this the Administrator stands up and leans her back against the glowing wall of the office, her arms outstretched like a scarecrow-Christ, and on contact with her skin the wall begins a vigorous pulsing and its membranous material begins to fuse with the woman's own. It grows from the wall, covering her until it is hard to tell where she stops and the building starts.

– But don't take long deciding, she says, her mouth now but an aperture in the lining of the room. The ship leaves within the hour, as soon as we find a new Captain. I'll be recommending you for re-integration, given your … and here she shoots a squirrely glare at Nyla … *condition*. But it's not guaranteed, of course, these things always take time. The profit, she tuts. The profit. I can't make any promises.

Then she recedes into the wall, disappearing into the fabric of the building itself, the room pulsing ever more violently until only her emaciated face is still visible, and, with a wet smack, she is gone.

Willard and Nyla are left, sitting alone. Willard first reaches behind him and, through his shirt, squeezes hard on the Captain's book tucked into his waistband, making sure it is still there. Then they both stand and look outside, where the sky hangs yellowed with dust, and then to the river, twisted and silent, leading back into the bowels of the glittering city of glass and, somewhere out past it all, to the Line – which seems but a strange dream impossibly far beyond.

VII

Part 2: On the Power of Waiting

2.1 Waiting and Suppression: Personal Reflections on Lining Up

The seeds of the solution I will now propose were first sown some years ago, when I landed in Caracas airport.

It was a brutal concrete concourse, large enough that it could hold half the world but miserable enough to deter them from wanting to see beyond. It was teeming. Snaking lines of people followed barriers with retractable cords, cutting back on each other again and again in torpid turn after turn and over it all, hanging from the part-suspended ceiling on thin wires, huge signs declaring: *We carry out checks on 100% of arriving passengers, to keep out immigrants who have no right to enter and to welcome those who do.*

I was hours in that dour chaos of corkscrewing lines. Shuffling forward, holding out my passport, tannoys repeating that illegals would not clear customs – but no one left, no one gave up or tried to cut in. I eventually reached the border guard who, on seeing my face, waved me through without even looking at my papers, and took to harassing a blond family behind me.

A day later, I found myself outside a café by Bolivar Square and this time observed a quite different type of line. I was drinking a coffee and trying to work out how I might walk back to my hotel rather than get the bus, as it was often violently overcrowded. The throng at the bus stop were, like me, almost exclusively tourists staying on the other side of Caracas, most of them tired and scorched after a day walking the sights and not inclined to walk another six sun-baked kilometres back to their accommodation. But the line waiting for the bus was much different to the ordered torture I'd endured at the airport, not so much a line at all as a semi-circular mass gathered around a pole. Such were the numbers waiting, being in the wrong place when the bus arrived would almost certainly mean not getting on, and so the crowd rippled and swayed as people guessed and second-guessed the exact paving stone where the doors might open.

When the bus did arrive, it stopped some five metres away from the designated marker, and the thin charade of order was then completely abandoned. People started to clamber on with no deference for those in front, pushing and shoving, poking with elbows and shoulders. This was all too much for one would-be passenger, a tall woman with an expensive haircut and three children in tow. I watched as her anger erupted and she launched into a spittle-flecked and expletive-laden tirade at both no one and everyone, before exhausting herself and collapsing in melodramatic sobs.

What had happened here? I wondered. Why had the line at the airport worked so well when this line had managed to release the hidden atavist from inside a previously mild-mannered woman? I wrestled with this question for days but couldn't make head nor tail of it, not until I happened upon a story published in a magazine on my flight back to Kinshasa.

2.2 A Case Study in Tapping Primordial Fear[4]

'Unexpected item in the bagging area,' says the one working machine.

You rescan the bottle of Prosecco.

'Beep.'

You put the bottle into the bag beside the expensive salsa and the corn chips. You usually buy economy, but not tonight. Because tonight you know that someone special will be calling to the door of your flat in just over ten minutes. In your mind, they are already naked and,

---

4. First published as 'The Warp Spasm' in issue 212 of *Sky Hooks*, Air Congo's in-flight magazine.

for a sliver of time, they look as good as only imaginary naked people can: no clear discerning features, just a blur of perfect and exquisite flesh.

But you wonder if this sense of anticipation will be like that day you arrived at work and looked in your lunchbox, only to find your sandwich was at home in the fridge. For the rest of the day you were unable to stop thinking about it. Oh how you had wanted that sandwich. But what if someone ate it before you got back? Or what if, by the time you got home, the tomato had sogged into the bread and ruined it? After salivating over its tomatoey goodness all day this would be too hard to take, so maybe it would be better if someone ate it after all. By degrees, you begin to fear wanting their perfect and exquisite blur too much and they instead begin to resemble a large, if denuded, tomato sandwich.

By now, behind your daydreaming, a line has formed and it's getting longer by the minute. A woman with a face like a barn owl is pretending to wipe her glasses clean while glowering at your back. A man with an uncanny resemblance to a beagle is holding a box of cornflakes and shuffling his feet. A few places even farther back, a vole-like chap is holding the hand of his mousy daughter and muttering to his ostrichy wife.

'Beep' goes the machine for the third time and, in your haste to bag it up, your hands become even clumsier than usual and the salsa rolls out of the bag.

'Unexpected item in the bagging area,' says the machine.

Not now, you think, *not now not now not now* – because to some of us there is simply nothing quite so beautiful as the knowledge that a moderately attractive office worker will soon ring our doorbell. And nothing quite so painful as the fear of not being there to answer.

Confusion begins to tickle you with long fingers. Why is this bottle so unexpected? It is a bottle of Prosecco, a green one with a white and stylish label. This is a small supermarket, with a wine section. Surely the bottle should be the very thing a self-service machine in this supermarket would expect? Oh, what a fool you were to dislike the surly shop assistant who used to work here! How you would welcome her gum-chewing disinterest now; how you would embrace her thinly veiled contempt for the job.

Clean goes the owl. Stare goes the beagle. Mutter goes the vole.

Comeoncomeoncomeon you say with a whole disapproving Farthing Wood behind you, before adding *Please*. You have been raised to be polite, even to obdurate electronic equipment.

'What is that person saying?' says Beagle Features.

'I'm not sure,' replies Barn Owl, 'something about cheese I think. I wish they'd hurry up.'

Beagle Features groans.

'Cheese? As well?' says Vole, not muttering any more. 'We'll be here all bloody day. I wish they'd stop talking to the machine and bloody buy something.'

'Beep' goes the Prosecco again.

'Unexpected item,' says the machine.

I know I know, you begin to say, but the machine adds 'in the bagging area' anyway. Try as you might, you cannot fathom the depths of the bottle's unexpectedness – although it is beginning to feel as if you have swum down in an attempt to do so and are now fast running out of air. Confusion's fingers have been usurped by the pinchy digits of frustration in the face of perceived electronic injustice. Pinch go the fingers. Pinch pinch pinch. You bang your forehead on the machine top.

'Look,' says Owl Face, 'they can't do that, can they?'

'Yes,' says Beagle Features, 'where's their decency?' and he shakes his head in disgust.

You are pretending not to hear them, but you cannot ignore their eyeballs devouring the back of your neck. You know how they see you. They see you as a crook, as a thief. These are not any old people you are holding up, they are *individuals*. They are all individuals, with hopes and dreams and places to be and aspirations that cannot be realised while they are stuck in this line. Who are you to take their dreams away from them? Do you think they are people who can afford to idle away their days in supermarket lines? They work hard. They pay their taxes. They don't deserve this. They most certainly do not deserve this. The hairs on their necks bristle and the line becomes a tinder-box, resting on a knife's edge. And all the while your watch ticks and the pinchy digits pinch on.

You move the corn chips to absolutely make sure that there is enough room in the bag for the Prosecco. Then you scan the bottle one more time.

'Beep,' says the machine.

You place the bottle into the bag and hold your breath.

Tick. Tock. The machine is silent.

Tick. Tock. And then it says … 'Unexpected item in the bagging area.'

Your anger froths out like milk boiling over. White rolls of rage bubble down you and puddle on the floor. You begin to beat the machine, swinging the packet of corn chips in wide and swathing arcs. *You cretinous mechanical moron!* you scream. *It's not a naked mole rat!*

In your anger you have forgotten that naked mole rats are neither rats nor moles but are actually a sub-species of porcupine. Maybe if you had remembered this, things would have worked out differently.

It's a bottle of wine, you shout, *and this is a super-market! I've scanned it five fucking times!* The machine blinks at you, pretending not to understand, but its silence enrages you further.

You begin to thrash the machine with a renewed vigour. The packet of corn chips bursts open due to the ferocity of the beating and triangular snacks go cartwheeling through the air. A spinning chip hits the owl-faced woman on the ear and she begins to tremor on the spot – quietly at first, like an electric toothbrush that has fallen into a sock drawer and accidentally switched itself on. But when a second starchy triangle hits her on the chin she explodes.

'Assault! Assault on that poor machine! Swearing and assaulting that machine, that innocent machine! Isn't someone going to do something?'

Righteous and owlish indignation shoots out of her and into the air like matches flicked into a field of dry grass. They rain down on the rest of the shoppers, who ignite, one by one, and go careening around the supermarket.

'The children, think of the children,' wails the ostrichy woman and she covers her daughter's mousy eyes.

'Oh my god, will you have some self-respect?' barks Beagle Features, shamed into action by Owl Face's outburst and his thin walls of stoicism tumbling down. He bites chunks out of his cornflakes box and begins to spit out mouthfuls of cardboard. 'Pull yourself together,' he says, 'you're embarrassing yourself. You're embarrassing all of us.'

A schoolboy who has been trying to buy a doughnut for the last twenty minutes shoots back off into the bakery section and begins to dismantle the shelving. A granddad with beady little eyes – and who had only come in to buy some breakfast biscuits – is carried along by the waves of mind-warping fury now sweeping through the supermarket. Being towards the back of the line, he does not fully understand what is happening – but he knows he doesn't like it. He has not fought in two world wars for this, definitely not for this, and so he begins to beat his walking stick on the floor. Unusually large tears begin to roll out of his eyes and had you been able to see him you might have wondered how a man with such small and moley eyes could produce such large tears. But he could.

You, however, know none of this because you are now encased in a hardening skin of gibbering insanity. You are now saying things that have no real meaning, like the barcode of an onion you remember from your days working in Roots 'n' Fruits. *36220000440*, you say, your mind no longer your own.

A librarian with a fully loaded basket has become unhinged by the slowness of the line and is now sitting cross-legged on the floor, submerging herself with the contents of her basket: custard, treacle, mayonnaise, pilchards, crème fraîche. She had only come in because of a hankering for carrot batons but had then, and quite inexplicably, filled her basket with things she never usually bought, things she didn't even particularly like. What a terrible day to fill her basket with such impulsive and slimy produce. What rotten luck.

The packet of corn chips is now completely empty, but you are still thrashing the machine for all you are worth. *36220000440*, you say.

'Unexpected item in the bagging area,' says the machine and you know that, right now, at this very moment, someone is ringing your doorbell. You see their index finger pressing the button and hear the buzzing echoing through the empty depths of your flat.

Or rather, you would see this if your mind had not left you. But it has. It has left you like students leaving a classroom when they realise that a teacher, whom they hitherto thought was merely late, is not in fact going to turn up at all.

You open the salsa. You apply it to your face like make-up. You fill your pockets with it. You throw it in the air like wet and gooey confetti. You are no longer human, you are now but a warbling barcode automaton, a salsa-smeared robot of despair.

'Unexpected item in the bagging area,' says the machine and by now the crowd is rabid.

Line-related hatreds have burst forth from their ids and are flying around the shop like ghosts escaped from inter-dimensional portals. Every occasion they have stood in a line to then at the very last minute be gazumped come flooding back: the memories of times when, after waiting so patiently, their counter had closed and another one had opened. They recall, aghast, how everyone behind them had run to the newly opened counter pretending to be innocent of what they were doing.

These memories make the shoppers behind you start to bay like coyotes, coyotes who wanted the blood of those who cannot line up, who will not line up, those who think it is OK to steal other people's precious time.

So, when you say *36220000440* again but still do not pay for anything, it is simply too much. The owl-faced woman punches you right on the ear and down you go like a teenager's zip. But the crowd cannot be sated so easily, no more than you could save yourself from a lion by throwing it a head of lettuce.

They tear into you. Beagle Features stabs you repeatedly with the keys of his cripplingly expensive house. The ostrichy woman skewers one of your eyeballs with her stiletto, shoes she wears for work not because they are comfortable but because not to do so would have hurt her career prospects. The mole-eyed granddad pulls on your left arm until it comes off and then swings it around his head. The voleish chap, releasing years of pent-up suffering at the hands of his gaslighting partner, bites off your nose. Children ransack your body. They dig through your abdomen with their little fingers, tearing out your organs and then squawking as they hold your gizzards up to the fluorescent lights. Never let someone steal your time, they seem to say with each fresh assault: never, never, never.

Eventually, when bits of you have been scattered cathartically all through the supermarket, the crowd begins to abate.

Blood-spattered shoppers forget what they had been doing. They pick themselves up, exchanging glances as might a man and his neighbour's wife upon discovering each other in a German pornography emporium. One by one, and without speaking, they begin to leave.

Men scuttle out the side exits and into the plaza, keeping their eyes on the floor. Women pretend to put on their make-up before following suit. Parents grab their children, adjusting their little collars and wiping slimy entrail residue away from their faces. Then they go out through the front and head off about their business – and all the while the machine sings on.

'Unexpected item,' it sings to your spleen as it sits on the scanner.

'Unexpected item in the bagging area.'

Part 3: An Elegant Solution

3.1 The Line: The Macroeconomic Case

That story helped make one simple axiom clear to me: a line has power.

An ordered line has the power to civilise, to keep us in check, and a disordered one the power to release our inner-primordials.

The 'line' by the bus stop in Caracas had a particularly powerful effect on that woman because it was so dysfunctional. In joining it she thought she was agreeing to a set of conventions, that she would put aside her selfish proclivities on the understanding that everyone else in the Line would do the same. And when this didn't happen? Then a terrible sense of injustice was released, an anger that the rules of the game had somehow been changed without her knowledge, something base had escaped from deep inside.

Yet lines are usually self-enforcing. Why?

It is because of something called 'line-homogeneity'. Even if all participants in a line aren't culturally homogenous, there is still usually a critical mass who are bound together by sharing a long-term stake in keeping the line working. Therefore, when lining up, most participants are prepared to accept an implicit (if not legally binding) etiquette to help keep the line ordered. But in Caracas, with so many tourists knowing they would never return, there was an absence of any such critical mass – and herein lay the weakness. The line in Caracas failed because not enough people were sufficiently invested in upholding a shared set of principles to make it work. The line was dysfunctional because of the extremely transient nature of its participants: it was comprised by a multitude, but few had any real long-term stake in seeing the project succeed. And that was when it became clear to me: how we choose to line up is really a reflection of our socio-economic psyche.

As any undergraduate textbook will tell you, economics, when reduced to the simplest principle, is the study of how the finite resources of the world are distributed to meet the infinite wants of humankind – and what is a line but a method of distributing a finite resource to a large number of people? Lining up is, then, economics in action. How people in (or from) a country choose to line up is a physical manifestation of the often-ineffable interactions between consumers and the economy, a country's economic zeitgeist made flesh.

At this point it might be tempting to think that in some places people don't line up at all – but that would be inaccurate. All societies have some system of lining up, no matter how chaotic it might seem to an outside observer. A society with no system of lining up (and here I mean none at all, no matter how implicit) would mean that anything – violence, murder, immolation – would be permissible as people waited for the distribution of a resource. But of course, outside of a failed state or cases of natural disaster or emergency, these things don't happen. And why? Because how we line up is an extension of the protective contract of common good between citizen and state, a reflection of what is elsewhere in society enshrined in legislature and enforced by a strong arm of governance.

And while the exact parameters of this contract change from place to place, inevitably defined and redefined by the particular socioeconomic conditions that prevail, once any form of contract exists so too does the blueprint for how people will stand in a line. In essence, a line is a society in microcosm; or, to put it in other terms, how we are governed decides how we line up.

Let us explore.

In Japan lines are ordered and quietly cheerful – they reflect the unfaltering faith that the Japanese have in the twin efficacies of large corporations and an infallible state. Lines in Japan reflect the social contract the Japanese citizen accepts at birth: *I approach even unpleasant social responsibilities with stoic good humour because, in return, I know things will run with utmost efficiency and everyone will be looked after.* Lines in Japan reflect the underlying certainty that everyone will reach, if not the top, then at least the place their social rank allows.

However, step just across the sea and things change. South Korean lines exist in a more semi-ordered capacity, at least by Japanese standards. People stand tightly packed, and line up in an orderly fashion – to a point. But, leave too big a gap and whump – there goes your place. Line-jumping is rife. People cut in, offering shameless justifications like 'I only have a quick transaction to make,' or 'I am running late for another appointment,' or simply, 'I am extremely busy.' Although this might seem rude to some looking in from outside, this phenomenon is explained by Korea's history. The pace of change since the end of the Korean War has reverberated across all aspects of Korean life, and lining up is no exception. The Korean line too reflects the transformative effects of flinging open the markets. Entrepreneurial spirit is now lauded in Korea – and everyone knows entrepreneurs do not waste time in a line (not successful ones anyway). A new social system has been born, one with a burgeoning upper-middle class. It is tacitly accepted that it may not make economic sense for an upper-middle-class Korean entrepreneur to wait behind a factory worker in a line; their time is so much more valuable. It is, after all, the Korean entrepreneur's nous which allows the Samsung salaryman to pay the mortgage.

This philosophy to lining up can be seen in Vietnam too, now that it has immersed itself fully in the waters of international investment. Here, lines tend to be more wedge-shaped than linear as people seek to gain advantage by sidling up either side and then cutting in at the last possible moment. Again, semi-recent Vietnamese history plays no small part. They have survived a brutal and crippling war and the terrible poverty of its aftermath. They are survivors, and survivors don't wait patiently in lines.

In the Asian super-giants of India and China, lining up becomes even less ordered. Lines are more like semi-ordered scrums, rough guides to where people should stand. This might seem barbaric to, say, someone from Kinshasa, but of course if you are born into a country with a population in excess of one billion, then you too will grow up with an acute appreciation that the devil damns the hindmost.

In America, or at least the America when people still lined up, etiquette was underpinned by the predominant belief that both success and failure are down solely to personal enterprise. Such a faith can be traced back through America's history too, to its puritanical roots and the belief that wealth accumulated was that which God has lent thee in recognition for good works. But such faith cuts both ways – if those who amass wealth do so as a divine reward for pious industry, then those who don't owe their poverty to fecklessness and sacrilegious indolence. And so American lines were often conducted with a veneer of bonhomie overlaying a crevasse-deep urge to grab a rifle; those at the back became desperate as their slovenliness was forever damned by both God and country – if getting to the top of a line was a validation of a person's good character, then not getting there was punishment for their ineptitude – and such desperate people often did desperate things.

Nodnol lines are – were – famously obedient and repressed. They were not enforced by assault rifles but by tutting. Irish lines are, as in so much else, a watered-down version of an inherited British formula; less efficiency but more cheer. Congolese lines are so efficient that skipping one is unthinkable, a rejection of the very fabric of African egalitarianism itself …

… and we could go on. But the point is clear. How we line up may change from country to country, from mindset to mindset, but it is always a function of how we have learned *to think*.

And if changes to how we think change the way we line up, then the reverse must also be true.

Changes to how we *line up* can be used to change the way our minds work.

3.2 The Line – The Microeconomic Case

Who hasn't stood in a line at some point? In a supermarket or to get into a cinema or a nightclub? Over your entire life, how much time have you spent waiting? Weeks? Months? Lining up is as much a part of life as cooking or watching television. But what could have been achieved in this time, had you not been waiting? Or, in economic terms, what was the opportunity cost of all this waiting?

An opportunity cost is the 'cost' of the 'opportunities' you forgo when you decide to do one thing instead of something else. It is the price economists place on that most peculiar and scarce of resources – time. Every decision we make has an opportunity cost attached: that is, if you choose to do X then you can't do Y; if you go to work, you can't spend that time with your family. If you order the pork, then you forgo the sea bass. An opportunity cost can be mitigated by increased access to other resources (for instance, if you have the money, and the appetite, then you can have the pork *and* the sea bass, and then the beef if so inclined), but the resource of time is economically peculiar because it is *universally* limited – no one has (or can have) more or less of it than anyone else. So why is it then that we choose to fritter so much of it away by idling in lines? To live is to line, it seems. However, what if we could make it the other way around?

Let us consider this by investigating what I have called the *Time Elasticity of Lining up* (TEL). The TEL of any line is useful as it can tell us how 'elastic' (or responsive) that particular line will be in relation to any change in the availability of the commodity for which that line has formed (which I will from herein call *Line Commodity Availability,* or LCA). In practical terms, 'elastic' means how quickly people will leave the line to go elsewhere should the commodity become more, or less, available. There is a generally (but not always – more on this later) a direct and inverse relationship between the availability of any commodity and the length of a line waiting for it: that is, as availability of a commodity decreases so we expect the length of the line waiting for that commodity to increase (and vice versa).

All lines we currently know of are 'imperfect lines'; that is, they are all responsive, to some degree, to changes in LCA. Therefore, all known lines fall into one of three types.

The first type of known lines are said to be *elastic,* and they exhibit a TEL > 1. These types of lines are the most common. They react to changes in LCA in the expected manner, but are *disproportionately responsive* to any increase (or reduction) in the availability of desired commodities. In these lines, people will readily leave if there is even a small restriction on the commodity for which the Line has been formed (or if the commodity becomes more easily available elsewhere). Examples of elastic lines might be people lining up for one particular checkout in a supermarket or people constantly changing lanes in slow-moving traffic. See diagram 1:

Diagram 1: TEL Curve for Positively Elastic Lines

*Here, even though a reduction in the availability of a commodity (from **R1** to **R2**) produces only a moderate increase in the length of the line (from **L1** to **L2**), this has a disproportionate reduction in the time people are prepared to wait (represented by the disproportionately larger decrease from **Ts1** to **Ts2**). This is due to availability of many possible alternatives.*

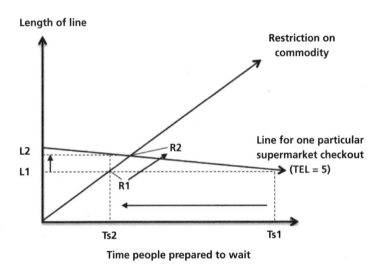

The second type of line is a little less common and exhibits an elasticity response of TEL < 1. These lines are said to be *inelastic* – that is, they still react as expected to any changes in LCA but are *disproportionately unresponsive*. In *these* lines, people will stay in line *despite* severe increases in restrictions of the commodity for which the line was formed, usually because the commodity is not readily available elsewhere. Examples of inelastic lines might be people lining up for concert tickets or for petrol during a shortage or, at the most inelastic, diabetics lining up for insulin during a war. See diagram 2:

Diagram 2: TEL Curve for Positively Inelastic Lines
*Although an increase in restrictions (from **R1** to **R2**) increases the length of line significantly (from **L1** to **L2**), this has comparatively little impact on how long people will wait (represented by the dis-proportionally smaller movements from both **Tc1** to **Tc2** and **Ti1** to **Ti2**). This is because there are very few alternatives available.*

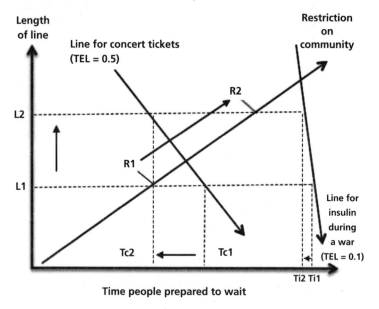

Time people prepared to wait

There is also a third, but much less common, type of line called a Veblen (or ostentatious) line. These lines also exhibit a TEL > 1 but are said to be *negatively elastic*: that is, they are *disproportionately responsive* to changes in LCA but the responses of these lines are the *opposite* of those of elastic lines. In these lines, *more* people will join the line the *longer* the line gets (although only up to a point). Although this might seem counterintuitive, anyone who has experienced a bouncer deliberately hold a line for a trendy nightclub to then find out it is actually empty inside will understand the rationale behind a Veblen line: some commodities are thought 'better' if the line for them is longer, and therefore a longer line sometimes attracts more people. See diagram 3:

Diagram 3: TEL Curve for Negatively Elastic Lines
*Notice that, initially, an increase in restrictions (from **R1** to **R2**) causes a moderate increase in the length of the line (from **L1** to **L2**), but this also increases the time people are prepared to wait (from **Tv1** to **Tv2**). This is due to the ostentatious value of the good. However, due to opportunity cost, at some stage (point A) the costs foregone by being in line overcome the good's Veblen effect, and so a positive elasticity is restored (the time people are prepared to wait reduces from **Tv2** to **Tv3** when restrictions increase to **R3**).*

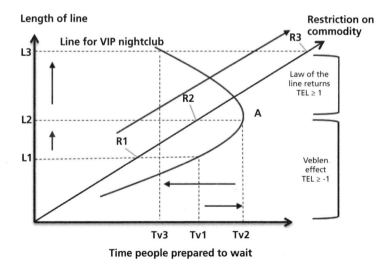

And why are all lines that we know of responsive to some degree to LCA?

Because of opportunity cost: at some point, no matter how desperate someone is to obtain a commodity, the negative effect of time spent in a line will outweigh the perceived benefit of reaching the top. Even a diabetic waiting for insulin will, at some point, decide they prefer the alternative of not getting it to another minute of waiting.

But what if we could engineer a 'perfect line', one that was impervious to succumbing to opportunity cost? One that was therefore *infinitely inelastic*, was *totally unresponsive* to any changes in LCA? Imagine if we could engineer a line people would *never leave* because they would never want to be anywhere else? One that people would wait in *forever* – even with only with little hope of ever getting to the end?

This would be a *perfect* line. It would be both perfectly terrifying and perfectly irresistible.

For within it would lie a perfect power: an ability, like no other, to control people by harnessing the power of waiting and tapping into their most latent and primordial fears.

3.3 The Power of the Perfect Line

Diagram 4: TEL Curve for the Perfectly Inelastic Line

*Here, an increase in length of the line (from **L1** to **L2**) initially has no reduction on the time people are prepared to wait (**TEL = 0**). There then becomes a time (point **X**) people have become so invested in waiting that any further increase (**L2** to **L3**) becomes infinitely negatively elastic (**TEL ≥ −1**) and therefore actually increases the time people are prepared to wait (to **T3**). Notice here, as there is never any real chance of achieving the commodity for which people are lining up, there is no 'restriction of commodity' curve.*

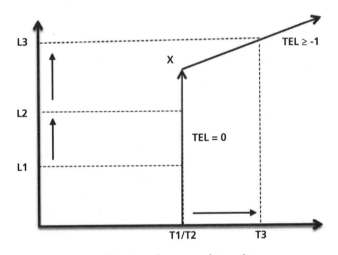

Time people prepared to wait

During the course of my research, I discovered that a near-perfectly inelastic line did once briefly come into existence.

It formed as people waited to cross over and back at checkpoints between Ukraine and Russian-held

Crimea.[5] Due to a serendipitous alignment of economic collapse, political instability and extreme social uncertainty, a number of people actually died rather than leave it. Such was people's desire to get to the end (or, and perhaps more accurately, such was their hopelessness at the alternatives of *not* being in the line) that they chose to die rather than lose their place.

But if a nearly perfectly inelastic line came into being *without any* planning or foresight, due only to a squall of socio-economic circumstance, then imagine what could be created *with* sufficient planning and resourcing?

With enough political will, a perfectly inelastic line could not only be *built* but also *maintained* – and maintained *indefinitely*. The world could have a line *that no one would ever want to leave.*

For the perfect line (from now called 'the Line') to exist, the following conditions would be needed:

1. The opportunity cost for an individual being elsewhere would need to be eliminated. This could be done by making the perceived benefit derived from reaching the end of the Line so 'good' that it would eclipse an infinite waiting time.

---

5. Documented by Olga Malcheveska in an article called 'Killer Lines of the Ukraine', which chronicled the plight of thousands of Crimean citizens who waited to cross into the Ukraine each week in order to receive their social welfare payments, before then lining up again to return.

2. In practical terms, there is no one 'perfect' commodity that will ever be perceived by every individual as being so beneficial as to negate all opportunity costs and forever. Therefore, the only 'thing' which could eclipse the entirety of an individual's opportunity cost would be their own *mythologised idea* of a 'perfect' commodity.

3. Thus, people would need to Line Up not in the expectation of definitely receiving their mythologised commodity, but only in the hope of *possibly* receiving it. This is because more utility will always be derived from the 'hope' of obtaining such a mythologised commodity than from obtaining the actual commodity itself. In essence, if someone ever got to the top, they would be disappointed – and word would then spread.

4. For this reason, the Line would have to be infinitely long.

5. The best solution, then, would be to construct a circular Line – and one of so large a circumference that no person could complete a full revolution in their lifetime. Perhaps around the perimeter of a very large country or continent.

6. To further ensure that the opportunity cost of leaving the Line is negated, the alternative to being in the Line would also need to be terrible – and conditions within the Line must be better than conditions outside.

7. In practical terms, conditions in the Line would need to be, at worst, tolerable, and the world outside would need to be so barren and hostile that leaving would mean almost certain death.

8. After a certain amount of time, the Line's inhabitants would shift their desires away from a specific idealised commodity and towards a more uniform goal: the generic and nebulous hope of 'reaching the top'. This is advantageous as nebulous and generic desires are favourable to specific and concrete ones; they are both easier to propagate and harder to disprove.

9. People would also need to fear losing their place. This fear could be accentuated by:
a) constantly hinting that they were close to the top;
b) making the Line so long that people would not countenance having to return to the start; and
c) making the time people spend in the Line span multiple generations.[6] In this way, people would

---

6. There is well-documented evidence pertaining to the strength of belief systems that reach a second generation of believers (and beyond) and so become established. One of the most comprehensive of these studies is that of Oni and Vaughan, who spent time studying the Cargo Cults of the Appalachian Mountains after *The Great Bubble* following the Chino-American Trade Wars. Oni and Vaughan witnessed how second-generation Appalachian communities, living in the mountains in isolation, had developed a belief system worshipping cargo aeroplanes. Oni and Vaughan documented how, never having seen a cargo aeroplane themselves but still 'remembering' stories passed down from previous generations (what Oni and Vaughan called a community's 'collective consciousness'), the Appalachians worshipped a deity called the Thunder-Hawk. They built runways (called 'lay-lays') out of decorated

feel indebted to family members/friends who had kept their place by Lining Up before them, and would not leave for fear of betraying these sacrifices (represented by point X in diagram 4).

10. There would need to be a small group of individuals within the Line with a vested interest in both maintaining tolerable living standards and in propagating the Line's mythology (thus keeping everyone Lining Up). These people initially should be planted by outside agencies, but removed as soon as feasible. For the Line to succeed in the long run, those with an interest in maintaining it would need to be indigenous. People most effective in this role would be predisposed to zealotry and authoritarian adherence to dogma, and they should be identified by algorithmic personality screening. They should then be 'given' positions of relative power and privilege within the Line to further consolidate their zealotry.

---

stones and poles of coloured cloth and prayed by making noises like a revving jet engine in the hope of placating the Thunder-Hawk. They believed that, once suitably appeased, the Thunder-Hawk would land on their lay-lay carrying both the messiah, a deity they called Colonel Greenspan, and a bounteous cargo. The most significant conclusion Oni and Vaughan drew from their research was that for a belief system to endure, it did not matter how often things *failed to happen,* only that a suitably large (and powerful) section of a community believed *it had happened once*. Oni and Vaughan called this seeming irrationality the 'evidence–belief paradox' – where *lack of evidence* paradoxically serves to *strengthen belief*. It is this paradox that will allow the Line to become most effective and self-regulating once the second generation of 'Liners' has been established.

3.4 The Perfect Line: How Big Data Can Build a Solution

We are faced with an intractable problem.

Our new model of Afro-Hispanic data-investment is currently driving an unprecedented growth in world GDP – but it is also inadvertently driving the migration patterns that threaten to wash the very stilts out from under the platform on which this new global prosperity stands.

So what can be done?

There are only two solutions. The first is, in truth, no solution at all and hardly bears countenancing: unplugging the magnet that is sucking European and American migrants towards the Tropics by turning off the whole system of data-finance. But this would be cataclysmic. It would lead to a total collapse of the world economy and a global recession on an unprecedented scale. Even conservative estimates put the minimum reduction in world GDP to more than 60%.

However, there is another option, a way we might kill the (by now rabid) goose but allow it to keep laying golden eggs, and it is this: to build an even bigger magnet elsewhere. A magnet that can be turned on and off at will, one that people will not leave, cannot leave, not unless someone wants them to. And I have designed that very magnet – it is called the Line.

For it to succeed, we must engineer the Line in two key areas:

1. Around the circumference of the barren deserts of Arizona and extending over the Rockies towards the Appalachians, possibly even as far north as the Great Lakes. This would be financed and then overseen by Mexico and Cuba.
2. Around the perimeter of mainland Europe, crossing the Alps and possibly extending as far east as the Ukrainian steppes. To be financed and overseen by a Pan-African alliance.

The process would need to be as follows:

1. A negotiation period between developed nations to finalise arrangements for funding, oversight and maintenance.
2. *Foundation phase.* Large-scale gathering (in key migrant hot-spots) of personal data from social media streams, in order to identify the specific 'ideal commodity' for which each person will be prepared to wait longest. User data to be gathered and stored.
3. *Early implementation phase.* Key social media channels used to target personalised adverts to *all* citizens in key migrant hot-spots. High-net-worth-high-skill (HNHS) individuals encouraged to migrate to developed countries (to help increase tax revenue and thus pay for the

Line). Low-net-worth-low-skill (LNLS) to receive individually targeted advertising about the Line on *all* social media channels. Each advert to be algorithmically tailored to an individual's specific 'ideal commodity' (as earlier identified).

4. Targeted advertisements will help individuals establish a 'personal mythology' about the Line, one that will then allow them to take ownership of their own idiosyncratic 'brand narrative'. In effect, this will help each individual cement the Line as a legitimate brand entity that, when it comes, dare not be missed.

5. *Mid-implementation phase*. In-depth algorithmic analysis used to identify suitable 'Elders' – those who will be needed within the Line both to propagate its mythology and to keep it running smoothly in the early phases. Extensive 'training' to be provided and an on-going remuneration package to be agreed between overseeing nations.

6. *Implementation phase*. The routes of the Line(s) decided upon. All areas 500km either side of the agreed routes rendered inhospitable through co-ordinated chemical interventions. All available media channels to present this as an apocalyptic event, all HNHS individuals to be evacuated and all LNLS urged to join the Line in order to survive.

7. *Maintenance phase.* Afro-Hispanic nations to provide on-going aid and materials (via air-drops) in order to ensure the Line has at least tolerable living conditions (and therefore maintains its status quo). Elders to be used to collect and disseminate aid in orderly fashion. Elders who keep their 'arc' of the Line in the most orderly condition to be rewarded with more regular and bountiful ration drops. During early maintenance, these rations could be used to develop internal reward schemes for those who approach the Line most enthusiastically (although the need for such rewards should diminish once the Line's mythology becomes established).

8. *Monitoring phase.* Once the mythology of the Line has been firmly established ('firmly' in this case means for at least one generation), it will become, in effect, self-policing. At this point we will have reached point X on diagram 4. People will now have invested so heavily in waiting that losing their place will be unconscionable. The Line will now need 'monitoring' rather than any real 'hands-on' management and maintenance costs will fall dramatically.

Conclusion

Overall, the paper finds that, if current world migratory patterns are not curtailed, then the global economy risks a complete collapse.

It does not recommend, however, exploring any solutions that might reduce current data-finance operations, due to the detrimental economic impact this would have.

This paper has identified a cyclical difficulty in trying to reduce Euro-American migration while still allowing global data-finance operations to continue, because it is the data-finance operations themselves that create these migratory by-products. Therefore, this paper concludes, the *only way* to stem current migratory trends without stopping global data-finance operations is by constructing a perfectly inelastic line (the Line).

This paper finds that the Line can be constructed quickly if supported with sufficient resources and planning. Although start-up costs will be high, they will soon pale into insignificance against the alternative costs of policing, enforcing and dealing with immigration in the long term.

Initially, the perfectly inelastic nature of the Line will need to be artificially maintained but, as a mythology is established, the Line's perfectly elastic nature will become self-reinforcing and thus costs will fall exponentially. Also, because major data-finance companies have already gathered much of the key data needed, start-up costs can be further ameliorated if an agreed network for co-operative data sharing can be established.

This paper also finds that, although the migratory by-products created by data-finance operations are currently a destabilising force, by building the Line migratory by-products will actually help *increase* stability. This is because data-finance firms could be allowed to draw from any stocks of capital held within the Line in order to fill periodic labour shortages. (This paper does recommend, however, that any drawing of capital from the Line be tightly regulated.)

Furthermore, allowing data-firms to draw from capital reserves stored within the Line would have two other advantages. Firstly, it would help keep labour costs low and thus act as a brake to domestic inflationary pressures. Secondly, it would allow rumours of people 'reaching the end' to spread around the Line, and so further establish the Line's mythology.

Of course, any capital stock taken from the Line could never return. Data-firms would need to give careful consideration as how to best utilise such resources when their needs for labour diminish.

Ben-Orkul, A. *Raising Capital – Razing Capitals*. Invisible Hand Publishing.

Bullough, O. *The Real Goldfinger: The Man Who Bankrupted Nodnol*. Article.

Brautigan, R. *Wendel and his Bowling Trophies*. Sunspot.

Choon, K. *23 Things They Don't Tell You about Data-Finance*. Smith & Ricardo.

Egaraf, N. *Lines: What Are They and Why Do We Bother?* Bell.

Keboun, R. *The Warp Spasm*. Sky Hooks #212.

Grogan, K., Lowry, A. and Brett, J. *Pretty Shitty Cities*. Comparative Advantage Publishing.

Grosney, Z. *Ben-Orkul – The Man Behind the Myth*. Article.

Malchevska, O. *The Killer Lines of the Ukraine*. Article.

Ohm, K. *An Introduction to Modern Data Finance*. Liquidity Press.

Oni, A. and Vaughan, T. *Enter the Thunder-Hawk*. Lorenz-Curve.

Stevens, W. *The Emperor of Ice-Cream, Harmonium*. Knopf.

Stiglitz, J. *Micro-Economics for the Mildly Nefarious: Ceteris Paribus and other Convenient Qualifiers*. Multiplier Books.

VIII

MORNING

Always before dawn come Nyla's calluses.

Willam feels her leathered palms scratching at his shoulder, rousing him. He smells the billy-fires. *Morning again*, he curses.

– Up, up, she says. Water. And the roof too, while you're about it. Up.

Willam tries to roll off, to disappear back into his ragged excuse for a blanket. Her hands disappear and he thinks he has won – but then she whips the blanket away, leaving him shivering naked under the dirty tarpaulin.

– Are we moving? he says, eyes still shut. I'm not getting up if we aren't moving.

– No, says Nyla, walking away.

A corner of the blanket is held tight in the crook of her elbow; the rest hangs down by her leg, too short to reach the ground.

– But I've heard rumblings, she says. A big shift. And coming soon. Very soon. Maybe today.

– That's what you said yesterday, says Willam.

– Hush, she says. Up.

Willam lies still, trying to hug himself back to warmth but attempting to keep the heat inside himself is like trying to stop water escaping a sieve – whatever bit of his body he wraps in his arms only makes the rest feel colder.

He gets up, pinching back both shoulder blades in an attempt to wring the stiffness from his back.

DRESSING

Dirtandshitandroutine.

Dress before the cold can cut strips off his back, hopping from leg to leg to spare his feet. Throw on his overalls and then get his boots, making sure he undoes the laces rather than standing his feet into them because he knows the back and forth of his heel causes the leather to pull away from the sole. Last time Willam's boots fell asunder he was barefoot for near on a month.

Break the skin of ice on the water bowl – five below to form it this thick – and brush his teeth with a finger, catching a nut of water between cupped hands and dousing himself so his chest clamps and forces out his breath like a clouded ghost. Get his only shirt on, dust off his mattress-board, fold it tightly around the blanket and tie it in place with the frayed length of red twine. Stack it all in the corner with the water bowl so everything is ready. Just in case.

Just in case the Line moves.

Just in case It moves.

Just in case It ever moves.

THE TENT

Willam shares the tent with his mother, Nyla.

Inside is a stove and a red plastic basin acting as the sink. Stacked neat as possible beside the basin are some cooking utensils: one tin plate, one mug and bowl, one de-handled pot, a frying pan, a spatula with four snapped laths and a rusty ladle. The stove is no more than a hollowed earthen pit covered by a chimney, and the chimney is no more than a rudimentary pipe made from a series of lightweight metal cylinders. Each cylinder is narrower than the one before so Willam can slot them together to form a funnel, the end of which he pokes through the tarpaulin – a futile attempt to take the smoke away when cooking and boiling water inside. The billy-fires are on hold until ration-drops resume.

And Willam knows something important about the chimney – that he must wrap it in a layer of hessian to try stop it touching the tarp. Mother has told him more than once how, when he was a baby, Mr Hummel burst into their flaming tent in time to drag her and Willam clear of the vengeful hissing of melting plastic raining down upon them. Willam was lucky, she says. She was too, even though she lost her sight. They survived.

His father didn't. Choked in his sleep by the fumes.

LATRINES

Hanging by its handle on the far side of the tarp is the small latrine shovel he and Nyla share with the other families. Willam walks out through the polythene flap and goes around to collect it. The head of the shovel is covered in a fungus of rust, bumpy and heavily stained, and is missing its handle. With the shovel in hand, Willam makes out for the latrine pits.

The latrine pits are near the tent line, in among the festering sprawl of the rubbish dumps. Many people don't bother making for the pits, just find a suitable rock to squat behind, but Willam remembers the last outbreak of dysentery, can still feel the retching of his stomach and wracking of the cramps. He always makes the journey.

The Line hasn't moved in a long time now, a long time, and pits are overflowing. The vomitous stink of purifying shit pours out of the half-dug holes and mixes with the stale ubiquity of the rubbish dump, and so Willard searches for a place to squat with the bottom of his shirt held hard against his nose.

At last he finds a small clearing. He digs a little, stops, sniffs and, satisfied, keeps digging. Then, hoping this time it will be solid enough to spare him sifting the rubbish for wiping-rag, Willard empties his bowels with a moan.

THE WALL

Willam stoops out through the polythene flaps of the tarpaulin. He knows Nyla has saved up fifty small-stone IOUs and he will need to take them up the line to buy some pap. But as he's getting ready, he hears a commotion. Not people going through their usual ablutions – but the dropping of plates, the pounding of feet and a frantic clamouring as whole families sprint up a nearby slope. Willam walks around the tarp and finds Nyla scrounging for tinder in the overflowing rubbish trench. He takes her by the arm.

– Come, he says, leading her by the elbow. Come.

They push up the crowded slope, Willam guiding Nyla, careful but insistent. The crowd gets thicker as they approach the brow of the slope, but Willam keeps pushing through until he can see.

– What is it? Nyla says, knuckling at her sightless sockets.

– It's a wall, says Willam. It's the length of the horizon and it's grey and it's huge. And there's something at the bottom. I can't quite tell – but it looks like a gate. I think they're letting people in.

ACKNOWLEDGEMENTS

Finishing this novel was made possible by the generosity of the *Society of Authors*, who awarded me a *Writer's Foundation Grant*. A very early – and almost unrecognisable – version of some of Parts IV and VI was first published in *Holdfast Magazine* as the short story 'Daedalus'. The section in Part V titled 'Africa "Creaking at the Seams" according to Kwoabo' was 'inspired' by a piece of rhetoric first published on the site infowars.com and then further spread on a number of Russian and Lithuanian websites. The mention of 'Killer Lines of the Ukraine' is based on an article 'Killer Queues of the Ukraine' written in 2019 by Olga Malchevska and published on the BBC World Service. The text on the sign in 'Caracas airport' is reproduced verbatim from a sign I saw on entering Gatwick airport in 2018. The section titled 'The Line: A Case Study in Primordial Fear' was first published in the

Galway Review as 'Unexpected Item in the Bagging Area', and then later as an appendix in *Did You Put the Weasels Out?* by Eyewear Publishing. The phrase 'let be be finale of seem' is taken from the poem 'Emperor of Ice Cream' by Wallace Stevens. The Captain's comment about 'all the love they bear you' is taken from the citizen's monologue in Shakespeare's *Coriolanus*, which I quote in full below. My brother Oisín first came up with the characters called moles – I owe him many a pint.

> *Care for us! True, indeed! They ne'er cared for us*
> *yet: suffer us to famish, and their store-houses*
> *crammed with grain; make edicts for usury, to*
> *support usurers; repeal daily any wholesome act*
> *established against the rich, and provide more*
> *piercing statutes daily, to chain up and restrain*
> *the poor. If the wars eat us not up, they will; and*
> *there's all the love they bear us.*

Thanks:
Thanks to Mum and Dad who taught me to value a book. If there is anything good in this one it belongs to you. An enormous debt of gratitude is owed to both my agent, Brian, and all the team at Tramp Press – Sarah, Lisa and Laura. Despite the romantic trope of the author

ploughing sole their lone furrow I am convinced, now more than ever, that writing is a joint venture, and without the repeated insights and unshaking belief of both my agent and my publishers this book would certainly not be as it is now (and probably would not have seen the light of day). Thanks to Nadine and Orla who, as ever, were patient and supportive of my indulgences in this project. Thanks to Mirelle and Roy, two of the biggest cheerleaders for my work – often more so than it has deserved. Thanks to everyone who has supported and encouraged my writing over the years and, although I hesitate to name just a few, a special thanks to Ben and Rich for encouraging even my more eccentric ideas; and to Andrew, who has read just about everything I've written and always found time to offer constructive advice – including the very insightful feedback he gave on an early draft of this novel over several frames of snooker in Edinburgh. Thanks again to Toby and Abi from the Loampit Vale writing group whose comments and advice on early scraps of this story were formative. Thanks to all who taught me at Goldsmiths, in particular Jack and Ardu, who both encouraged many of my early and more florid displays.